HOCKEY

DREAMS

BY

Gil Conrad

www.scobre.com

Scobre Press Corporation
2255 Calle Clara
La Jolla, CA 92307

First Scobre edition published 2005.

Edited by Anne Greenawalt
Illustrated by Gail Piazza
Cover Design by Michael Lynch

ISBN 1-933423-45-5

www.scobre.com

HOME RUN EDITION

CHAPTER ONE

NEW SKATES

I am sitting on a stool in an NHL locker room. I can't believe this is happening. Tonight, I will play in my first professional hockey game. At five foot six, and just over 160 pounds, I am very small, probably the smallest player in the league. That won't stop me, though.

A few of the older guys are looking me over. They look very calm as they prepare for another long NHL season. I recognize most of these players. After all, I've been cheering for this team since I was in diapers. Being around these guys is much different than watching them on TV, though.

My eyes dart around the room. I notice a few guys putting tape on their sticks. I see others listening to music. I even see one who seems to be asleep. After taking a deep breath, I pull on my game jersey.

A chill runs down my spine. I'm actually in the locker room of the Minnesota Elk. All the people who told me I was too short, too skinny—they were all wrong. In twenty minutes, my lifelong dream will come true.

I grab a pair of new skates from my locker. The blade at the bottom is shiny and sharp. I run my finger along it. Then I close my eyes, remembering my first pair.

I was just seven when my parents bought them for me. They were black and white with blue laces. I still have them today. They had been in the display window at a sporting goods store in town. Every time we passed by, I would ask Mom to *please* buy them for me. She'd always tell me the same thing: "Hockey is too dangerous for such a little boy, Wayne."

I grew up in the town of Robbinsdale, Minnesota. Hockey is a very big deal in Robbinsdale. Second grade was the first year of youth hockey. I would beg Mom to sign me up almost every day. Hockey flyers littered our house. I would bring them home from school every day. I put them up with hockey magnets on the refrigerator. I stuck one under Mom's pillow. Dad would find them in his briefcase, too.

With constant pressure, Mom finally caved in. When she handed me my new skates, a signed consent form was stuffed in the left one. I was going to play hockey.

Lacing my new skates up on the living room

floor wasn't easy. Dad warned me about how important it was to lace my skates correctly. If I missed a loop or twisted the laces, the skates wouldn't work right. So I really took my time. I pulled the laces through the tiny holes slowly. Dad repeated himself while I laced: "Hockey starts with your feet, Wayne. Great hockey players have great balance, great feet."

Jack Miller, my father, lived and breathed hockey. From the time I was a baby, he breathed it into me. "Hockey requires talent—that's true. But the best players aren't always the most talented. They're the guys with the biggest hearts. A great hockey player never quits, Wayne."

Putting on my new footwear was difficult. The skates were tight and uncomfortable. Hockey skates are different than figure skates. They are sturdy and heavy, even a bit clunky. The sharp metal blade is supported by thick plastic. The tongue is huge, too. And the high ankle support is hard to get used to.

"Do they fit?" Mom asked.

I tried not to show the pain on my face. Then I struggled to wiggle my toes for Mom. "Yeah, I think so."

Honestly, I didn't care how they fit. All I cared about was getting on the ice. I wanted to skate like Wayne Gretzky. Gretzky is widely known as the greatest hockey player of all time. My parents, who grew up in Canada, had been Gretzky fans since before I was born. When they learned they were having a boy, they named me Wayne right away. Before I was even born, I had a lot to live up to.

Once the skates were on, I tried to stand. I was unsuccessful. The blades dug into our carpet. This caused me to lose balance. I fell flat on my back. But first, I smacked my head on the side of the couch. I was frustrated, but I got back up. I was too excited to stay down.

A moment later, I was begging my parents to take me down to Mickey's. Mickey's Ice Arena was *the* place to play hockey in Robbinsdale. Dad was going to meet some friends there that night. I asked him to please let me go along with him. It didn't matter if I only got to skate for ten seconds. I just had to try out my skates on the ice—that night.

It didn't take much for them to let me go. Mom wanted to come, too. She wouldn't miss watching me skate for the first time. When we hopped in the car, my legs felt numb. The tightness of the skates around my ankles was killing me. Still, I couldn't stop smiling.

We made our way through the streets of Robbinsdale. The town I was born in was hockey-crazy. We had two hockey stores and three ice rinks downtown. That didn't include the rinks at the middle school and the high school. Plus, we played pond hockey from late October through March. Nobody played hockey during Minnesota Elk games, though. They were all glued to their TV sets.

The NHL franchise is located in the city of Saint Paul, just a few minutes away. Sure, we rooted hard for our football and baseball teams. When it came to hockey, though, we were fanatics. We went nuts for the Elk.

The drive from our house to the ice rink took about ten minutes. It felt more like thirty. I simply couldn't wait to get out there. When we pulled up to Mickey's, my heart jumped. Sure, I had been on the ice a few times before—but never in skates. That was because I hadn't owned skates until an hour earlier.

I looked over at my mother and she smiled. She shut the car off and said, "Now, Wayne, this is your first time out there. Promise me you'll take it slow." I had a history of being a little too fearless in my life. Like the time I rode my bike down an ice-covered hill in Lion's Park. I hit a bump, flew over my handle bars, and broke my arm. Mom already looked worried.

"I promise," I said with my smile spreading from ear to ear. Then we made our way inside.

We set up near center ice. Once there, we sat in folding chairs just outside of the rink. Dad waved as he grabbed his stick and jumped onto the ice. Although I loved watching him play, tonight was different. Tonight was going to be my turn. I could hardly stay in my seat. I wanted to get out there.

Dad was skating so fast that he looked like a blur. I honestly had a hard time seeing him as he flew by. At six feet four inches tall, Dad is big and powerful. But he's fast, too. He had been a forward for his high school team. During his junior season, he set a Canadian scoring record. There's a really cool plaque up at his high school with his name on it.

If things had gone differently, he would have played in the NHL. But then he broke his leg—really badly. The sad part was that it happened at the end of his senior season. Just like that, his NHL dreams fell apart. Dad sat in a wheelchair for a year. Eventually, he was able to walk again. By that time, though, his window of opportunity had closed. Hockey became his hobby, but was no longer a career option.

These games at Mickey's were something he did for fun. That didn't mean he didn't take them seriously. During league games, a different side of my father would come out. He was a tough-as-nails athlete—a warrior. Although well past his prime, he could still play the game extremely well. I wanted to play like him some day, but even better.

I shook my leg impatiently. I couldn't wait another second to get out on the ice. Just when I was about to explode, the game paused. Dad spoke to one of his teammates. "Phil, let's call it a night, okay? Little Wayne got a pair of skates. He's gonna try 'em out for a bit."

Dad skated toward me, pushing off the ice with smooth and powerful movements. When he was about five feet from Mom and I, he stopped short. He pushed his skate into the ice. This motion shot a thin mist of snow right at my face. I wiped the snow from my eyes and laughed. Then Dad grabbed me, lifting me in the air and over the boards. He planted me on the ice carefully. Once there, I held his shirt for balance.

Even though I was just seven, I'll never forget standing there on the ice. I'll never forget how the slippery surface felt beneath the blades. I couldn't understand how Dad moved the way he did. I couldn't imagine being in control like that on the ice. It was too slippery. The blade was too thin. My ankles kept rolling. And I hadn't even tried to skate yet! This didn't make sense. How was it possible to stay balanced? All of my weight was leaned on a blade no thicker than the point of a pencil. How was I ever going to be good at this?

I never had the chance to answer those questions. In a flash, Dad grabbed my hand and started to skate. "Hang on to me!" he yelled.

Then he took off, pumping his legs and moving his arms. For a forty-year-old, he was lightning fast. We started at center ice and made our way toward the far goal first. "Do you want me to slow down, Wayne? If you're scared, I can."

My sense of adventure had taken over. "No way," I yelled. "This is great! Go faster!"

"Faster? Okay, here we go." Then he *really* took off. We skated from goal to goal at full speed. My brown hair blew back from my face in the wind. I was really skating! Well, my father was skating—I was coasting. Still, it felt amazing! I held tight to Dad's jacket. The thin blades on my new skates kissed the ground below them. They barely made contact with the ice.

"Yeah!" I yelled at the top of my lungs. "I'm flying!"

Mom watched us closely from outside the rink. Once in a while, she would yell "slow down!" Dad kept skating with me hanging on tight. Occasionally I slipped, but I was always scooped up by my father. He never stopped moving or lost his balance—even for a second.

After about ten minutes, we reached the far goal. Dad stopped. Beads of sweat had formed on his forehead. With his hands resting on his knees, he told me to try skating on my own. So I did. Skating was not easy. I never got more than a few feet without falling. I was hooked right away, though.

"Stay right here," Dad said, skating back to the far goal. There, two hockey sticks lay on top of the empty net. He grabbed them both and made his way back toward me. Then he handed me a stick that was much too big for me. He dropped a puck. I slowly skated until I was about twenty feet from the goal.

"Take a shot, Wayne. Shift your weight back, and then forward when you hit the puck. Stay low. Make sure to hit the ice before the puck. Oh, and snap your wrist on the follow-through." I looked back at him with one eyebrow raised. "Just hit it," he said.

I took a deep breath. Then I zeroed in on the goal as I tried to stay balanced. I imagined myself being a professional with an open shot. I bent my knees the way I'd seen Wayne Gretzky do. I gripped the giant stick with two hands. Then I reached back and swung at the puck with all of my might.

Because the stick was so long, I lost my balance. I fell backwards. Amazingly, I still connected with the puck. Dropping my stick to the ground, I hit the ice with a loud thud. My head banged on the hard glassy surface.

I lay there on the ice, feeling a bump form on my head. Mom ran out to see if I was okay. She yelled at my father as he skated over. While rubbing my head, she blocked my view of the goal. My eyes welled up with tears, but I fought hard against crying. "Are you okay, sweetheart?" Mom said, kissing the bump on my head.

"You alright, champ?" Dad followed. "Keep your balance next time. I liked the way you snapped your wrist, but you have to focus on the . . ."

"Jack!" Mom interrupted. "He just hit his head. Give him a second." Dad never stopped coaching me.

A single tear streamed down my cheek. Dad lifted me back up to my feet. Once there, I looked over his shoulder and through my tears. There, sitting in the corner of the goal, was the puck. I'd made it.

A huge smile swept across my face.

CHAPTER TWO

LITTLE WAYNE

The Minnesota Elk locker room is awesome. The ceiling is high, and the floor is covered with soft green carpet. There is a big Elk logo in the center of it. I continue looking around the room. To my left, there are four flat screen TVs! Not to mention two vending machines that don't ask for quarters. This place is like an amusement park for hockey-junkies.

We're playing the Chicago Firestorm tonight. They are supposed to be good this year. Coach Lewis comes into the room to go over some last-minute strategy. I listen extra closely as he talks. He is writing a few things down on a dry-erase board in front of us. I take a mental note of every word he says.

Like my father, I am a forward. A few months earlier, I was a draft pick of the Minnesota Elk. I was the seventeenth player selected in the second round. In terms of the Elk's expectations, I don't think there are too many. I know the odds are against me. Many guys drafted in the middle of the second round don't stay in the NHL long.

I believe I am going to make an impact in this league, anyway. It's going to start tonight. Coach leaves the room and I continue to put on my gear. I drop my left shin pad onto the floor. One of the older guys, forward John Simpson, walks toward me. He takes his stick and slaps my shin pad over to Alexi Kornikov. The large Russian laughs, and shoots my pad back to John.

I stand up, not willing to let the older guys mess with my stuff. Being bullied is something I remember too well from my childhood. I know that I have to put an end to it right now. I make eye contact with one of my new teammates. Suddenly, I remember a time in my life when I was in a similar situation.

Entering middle school was a challenge for me. The kids were older, school was harder, and I was still tiny. Plus, on my first day of school, my locker got stuck. No matter how hard I pulled, it simply wouldn't open. This meant that I couldn't get my science book out. I was going to be late to my second period class.

I stood in front of the locker, chewing on my nails. The late bell rang loudly. The hallways quickly emptied out. Ten seconds later, I was alone. Sweat began to form in my armpits. *I can't show up late for my first day of class,* I thought. I pulled at the locker again, this time with all my strength. It wouldn't budge. I couldn't get a good enough grip on the door.

Then a light went on in my head as an idea occurred to me. I took the shoelace off of my right shoe. I tied it around the handle of my locker. Then I pulled and tugged on the lace. I used every ounce of strength I had. Finally, it gave. The locker door broke open with a loud crash. I fell backwards, with the shoelace still in my hand. Attached to the shoelace, was the dangling metal door of my locker. I had torn it clear off the wall.

Rattled by my broken locker, I dropped the metal door into a garbage can. My shoelace was still attached to it. Finally, I grabbed my book and sprinted to class. In rushing off, I grabbed the wrong book. My science book wasn't the only yellow book in my locker. My English book was yellow as well.

When I walked into class, everyone was staring at me. I must have looked pretty stupid. I was carrying my right shoe under my arm. And I was sweating from head to toe.

A few minutes later, things had calmed down. I was in my seat, taking notes on the layers of the earth's crust. Everything seemed okay. Everyone had stopped staring. Unfortunately, Mr. Weathers called on me to read. I quickly let him know that I'd left my science book in my locker. "I accidentally brought my English book." I said. "They're both yellow."

Mr. Weathers didn't seem to care. He stared at me as though I was a criminal. Then he pointed me out to the class. He said that I appeared to be a "disorganized little fella." He hadn't finished either. "Succeeding in this class without the proper books is impossible." Once again, everyone was staring at me.

The "disorganized" part didn't bother me half as much as the "little fella." I was definitely small—probably the smallest boy in school. That didn't mean I needed to be reminded about it all the time. It was bad enough that everyone I knew called me "Little Wayne." This nickname was something that had been with me since I was a baby.

I survived the next few periods. I got a new shoelace, and a new locker, too. When I headed to the cafeteria, my day was starting to improve. I was going to get through this after all.

In the pocket of my sweatshirt, I held my lucky hockey puck tightly. It was the same puck I had first scored with when I was seven. I carried it with me wherever I went. I loved that puck. It usually brought me good luck. On this day, though, it did just the opposite.

The school cafeteria was shaped like a giant square. There were about fifteen tables spread throughout. Sitting alone was as bad as it got for a middle school kid. When I saw my best friend, Ricky Vang, I sighed with relief. "Quick Rick" had already gotten his lunch and was halfway through it. The funny thing was, Quick Rick wasn't quick at all on the ice. He was actually pretty slow. He did everything else fast, though. Like getting dressed, lacing his skates, or eating a burger. It was a perfect nickname for him.

I walked over to the lunch line and grabbed a plastic tray. Then I piled on spaghetti and meatballs. From the corner of my eye, I noticed a group of familiar-looking guys. Darius Gray, Javier Cervantes, Mike DePeppo, and Brock Landon were the most talented hockey players in school. They were all eighth graders. They were all big and bad. Especially Darius.

Darius Gray was the star of the middle school hockey team. He was also well-known for being mean. He was a foot taller than me with a broad chest and big muscles. I stood in line, not noticing that I was staring right at him. Unfortunately, he *did* notice. "Can I help you with something?" Darius's voice was loud.

"What?" I asked, totally confused.

"Why . . . are . . . you . . . staring . . . at . . . me?" he asked.

"I . . . I wasn't." My heart raced as I answered.

He took a few more steps toward me. Then he grabbed a tray and piled food onto it. "I'm in a hurry," he said, explaining why he'd cut in front of me.

I didn't respond. I just let him cut. As we waited, he pointed to my Minnesota Elk sweatshirt. "You a hockey fan?" he asked.

"Yes," I answered. I was kind of excited that the hockey star was speaking to me. Maybe he had seen me play. Maybe he was excited about the chance for me to be his teammate. That is, if I made the middle school team. "I play, you know. Last year I started at forward on the. . ."

"*You* play?" He started laughing. The idea of me playing hockey was the funniest thing he'd ever heard.

"Yeah," I answered, trying to sound tough. "I'm going out for the team, too. So I'll probably see you at tryouts."

He called over to Javier. "Javy, come over here and meet this guy. He thinks he's making the team."

Giant Javier Cervantes, came barreling over to us. He looked at me, laughed, and bumped knuckles with Darius. "I've eaten sandwiches bigger than you, little man. Maybe you could be our mascot!" He held his stomach as he laughed. That was the second time I'd been called little in the past two hours. It really ticked me off.

At this point, most of the kids in the room were staring at me. I wanted to disappear. Instead, I said the dumbest thing possible: "You're right, I am little. But I'll knock both of you into the boards so hard you'll be seeing stars."

"What did you say?" Javier took a big step toward me.

"You heard me. I said I'll knock you out when

it counts. On the ice."

I braced myself to get punched. Then the woman at the cash register spoke, "That'll be one dollar and seventy cents, please."

Javier was so close to me that I could taste his lunch. Darius was standing directly to his left. I was cornered. Everyone in the cafeteria was staring. They all wanted to see the little guy get knocked out by giant Javier. I wondered how I was going to reach my seat without getting killed. I thought about making a run for it. Either way, after today, I was probably going to have to change schools.

"A dollar seventy, Hon," the woman behind the register repeated. I was holding up the lunch line.

Javier and Darius just stood there. They, too, were unsure of their next move. Hockey stars or not, they couldn't beat me up in the middle of the cafeteria. They would get into trouble for that.

"If you don't have the dollar seventy, you need to step out of line."

"Sorry," I said, finally reaching into my pocket. "My money is . . ." In the middle of this sentence, something awful happened. When I grabbed my money, my lucky puck dropped from my pocket. It hit the floor and spun there. As fast as I could, I reached down to grab it. I wasn't fast enough, though. Javier put his hand on my shoulder, stopping me cold. Of course, Darius saw this as a golden opportunity.

He grabbed the puck and gave me a nasty smile.

"You're dead at tryouts, little man. I can't wait." Then he walked back to the "cool table."

The woman behind the register handed me back my thirty cents change. I made my way over to Ricky's table. It was in the corner of the cafeteria. As I walked toward him, fifty sets of eyes were staring at me. Talk about a bad first impression.

I sat down next to Ricky.

"That went well," he joked.

"I can't believe I dropped the puck." I said.

"You just started a fight with the two biggest kids at school."

I didn't pay attention to his comment. Instead, I kept looking over his shoulder at Darius. My eyes were locked on my puck. "I want my puck back."

"Forget it, Wayne. Your puck is gone."

I stared down at my plate. Then I picked up one of the golf ball sized meatballs. I stuffed the entire thing into my mouth. I glared over at Darius—and chewed and chewed and chewed.

Ricky tapped my shoulder. "Dude, stop doing that."

I kept chewing.

"Stop doing that! Fighting with the hockey team is one thing. Grossing out the girls is another. I have to draw the line somewhere. Don't make me take away that second meatball."

I swallowed hard. I knew exactly what I had to do next. "I'll be right back. I have to get my puck."

With that comment hanging in the air, I stood up. Then I started my walk over to them. My heart was thumping.

Darius stood up when I got close to their table. He took my puck from his pocket. Then he began tossing it up into the air and catching it.

"Will you please give me my puck back?" I asked, nicely.

"Don't be such a jerk, Darius. Just give him his puck back." Jennifer Davis said.

"This is my puck, Jen." Darius answered, flipping the puck up again. "I found it on the floor." He got real close to me. My nose was in his chest. "You can't leave things on the floor like you don't want them, dwarf."

"I do want it. You saw me drop it. You know it's mine." Darius wasn't going to *give* me back my lucky puck. I was going to have to take it. Still, I asked one last time. "Please Darius, just give it back. That puck means a lot to me."

That was when Darius started to yell. "The puck is mine! You must be the dumbest kid I've ever met. Get lost!" he said, pushing me backwards.

There are moments in life when you pass the point of no return. This was one of them. Darius Gray was now my enemy. There was nothing I could do to reverse that. If he was going to hate me anyway, I might as well get my puck. So I did the only thing I could think of. I grabbed a handful of spaghetti and meatballs from Jennifer Davis's tray. Then I threw it in Darius's face.

What happened next was predictable. Darius knocked me to the floor with a right hook. He wasn't finished either. He then stuck his foot on my chest, holding me in place. Before I knew it, I was covered in Jennifer's lunch. Then he grabbed Javier's lunch. He poured that on my head too.

As Darius poured Brock's milk onto my face, Mr. Weathers came over. He yelled at Darius, then at me. We both ended up in detention for the next two days. That was the bad news. There was some good news, too: when he covered me in food, Darius dropped my puck.

I put it back in my pocket before being taken to the principal's office.

CHAPTER THREE

TRYOUTS

I can feel my blood beginning to boil. My new teammates continue to slap my pads around the locker room. Finally, Alexi Kornikov notices me standing. I am staring right at him. He can sense my anger. He is about to smash down on my shin pad. Our eyes meet and the strange Russian laughs. "Okay, I leave it alone. I can tell that you mean—I like mean." He then lifts up my shin pad and gently tosses it to me. "I'm mean too," he smiles.

"Thanks," I say, sitting back down. A sense of relief rushes over me. I may have just made a friend. I finish taping, and bending my stick. My goal is to get just the right amount of curve. I glance into my locker at ten more sticks. They are all mine. Tonight, I will begin my NHL career. There will definitely be some broken sticks along the way. I'm sure there will

be some broken bones as well.

A moment later, I hear a voice: "Five minutes, guys." Right away, my stomach fills with butterflies. We are about to take the ice.

Twenty-two players make up our team. In hockey, most players get into every game. This is extra exciting for rookies. We know we'll be seeing ice time from day one. Line changes will occur throughout the game. This means that players on the ice will rotate, again and again. This rotation is constant. Unlike basketball, football, or baseball, play does not stop. Players enter and exit the game during live play. Line changes are fast. Timing them just right is important.

I am considered an offensive sub—a player without a true role. Being a rookie, I am not on the first or second line. Coach has assured me that I am going to get in there. He just doesn't know when. This is why I have to be at full attention during the game. At any moment, my number can be called.

All of my gear is on. I stand up, stretching my back and my knees. I'm nervous, but filled with confidence at the same time. Following my teammates, I make my way down the long tunnel. This path leads us into the heart of the arena. I have been waiting for this my entire life.

I am in the middle of the pack. I take a deep breath when I first see the bright lights. "Here we go," I whisper.

The spaghetti incident was an awful way to start middle school. By the time I got home, I was sticky and gross. Not to mention smelly. I went straight to the laundry room. I looked over my shoulder as I undressed. I had to make sure my parents didn't walk in. There was no way I would be able to explain what happened. I dropped my jeans and sweatshirt into the washing machine. Then I threw in some laundry detergent.

With thirty minutes left before Mom got home, I jumped into the shower. I scrubbed tomato sauce out of my hair. I picked tiny pieces of meatball from the inside of my ears. It was disgusting.

After my shower, I walked into my bedroom. I stood with my back to the wall in the doorway. I had been making marks on that wall since my first day of kindergarten. I leaned my head back, and made a line with a pencil. I was pretty sure that I had grown. After all, it had been a full year since I had made my last mark.

This can't be right, I thought. The line I drew was directly on top of last year's line. I hadn't even grown a quarter inch! I stood at four feet four inches tall—again. I snapped the pencil in half and left my room.

The next week at school was okay. Sure, Darius wanted to kill me. But the spaghetti incident didn't turn out to be as terrible as I had thought. Some kids told me how cool it was that I stood up to Darius Gray. A few girls even talked to me, and that *never* happened! My big mouth may have actually paid off for once.

Ricky, on the other hand, was scared stiff. He and Darius had lockers that were pretty close together. About ten times a day, Darius would harass my best friend. He would push Ricky and tell him that he was dead at hockey tryouts. I felt terrible for Ricky. It was my fault. I had dragged him into this. It didn't matter that I hadn't meant to.

By Friday, Ricky was walking around with a limp. He told me that he had hurt his ankle. I didn't buy that for a second. I knew he was faking it. On Monday, he told me that he wasn't going out for the hockey team. I tried to convince him that Darius was just talking, but he wouldn't listen. Honestly, I wasn't sure that I even believed myself.

I wasn't scared of taking a few hard hits from Darius. I just hoped it wouldn't affect my chances of making the team. I thought I had a decent chance. After all, I had started at forward last season. That was elementary school, though. The competition this year was going to be much tougher. That wasn't going to stop me from trying out. Neither was Darius Gray.

Tryouts started on Monday afternoon. About forty kids showed up to earn one of eighteen spots.

We had one day to show off our skills to Coach Nielson. Coach was a huge man who never stopped blowing his whistle. I had known him for most of my life. He'd played hockey with my father at Mickey's. Dad used to say that he was the toughest guy he'd ever played with. When Coach Nielson spoke, we all listened.

At the beginning of tryouts, the guys lined up at center ice. I stood on the tips of my skates. I stuck my neck out to make it look like I was taller. Sam Bernard was the second shortest guy on the ice. I made sure to line up next to him. Coach skated around us. He nodded his head at me. *Great*, I thought, *he remembers me*. I had seen him play many games during my life. I was glad that he had seen me, too. Still, I knew that wasn't going to get me on the team.

The tryout was very simple. Coach divided us into teams of six players. Two teams played each other for seven minutes. Then we rotated. My team was made up of myself, three seventh graders, and Brock Landon. Brock was one of the top forwards on last year's team. Just my luck—we played Darius's team in the first game.

During our pre-game stretching, Darius, Javier, Mike, and Brock were whispering among themselves. They were looking directly at me while they stretched. I saw some pointing and heard laughing, too. Darius punched his hand hard. I flinched when I heard that. I tried not to look scared, but I was.

Coach Nielson dropped the puck ten minutes

later. I was playing right wing—directly opposite Darius. The moment the puck was dropped, he came after me. He didn't know how fast I was, though. I skated past him and broke toward the goal. I flew up the ice, knowing that nobody would be able to catch me. Our center noticed my run and smacked me a perfect pass. Before the defense closed in, I took a shot on goal. The puck hit the right post. I had just missed!

Their right defenseman controlled the puck. He skated up the right side. I recovered, skating back toward center ice. Brock was playing left wing and managed to steal the puck back. I flew down the center of the ice again. Brock saw me and made his pass. It was behind me, though. When I turned my body to get it, Darius flew in and crushed me. His body check was powerful. I fell to the ground hard. Darius took off down the ice, finishing with a goal.

I stood back up and took a deep breath. Brock was laughing. I wondered if he and Darius had set me up for that hit. "Something funny, Brock?" I asked.

He didn't answer.

Now I knew for sure that these guys were going to be teaming up on me. Even Brock, who was supposed to be on my team. All I could do was play my heart out. And I did. A few minutes later, I made another nice run at the goal. I took a slap shot that was barely saved. In terms of offense on our team, I was it. Brock was a step slow and totally scared of

Darius.

Darius followed me all over the ice. He punished me with one check after another. He must have knocked me down ten times during that seven minute game. There wasn't much I could do about it either. He was two years older than me, strong, athletic, and fast. Plus, he was mean.

"Thirty seconds, guys," Coach said.

Darius took a shot and our goalie made a kick save. He passed it up the right boards. I reached my stick out and got it. I took off with one man between me and the goal. The defender started to skate at me. He was gearing up to deliver a body check. I put my shoulder down and pumped my legs. I wasn't backing down.

As I got closer to him, I changed my mind. I stopped short. Then I spun around so that he skated right past me. It was my best move of the game. When I looked up, it was just me and the goalie. Quickly, I reached back. Shifting all of my weight onto my back foot, I lifted my stick high into the air. I had a clear shot on goal.

From nowhere, though, Darius came flying in. I never even saw him. While I was in my backswing, he laid into me. It was a clean hit that knocked me to the ice. I never got the chance to hit the puck. I lay on the floor, and had to be helped off the ice.

"You okay, Miller?" Coach Nielson asked me.

Darius had knocked the wind out of me. I wanted

to speak, but nodded my head instead.

"Next two groups!" Coach blew his whistle. Twelve new guys skated onto the ice.

I sat on the bench drinking from a water bottle. My head hurt, my chest hurt, and my legs hurt. I could feel Coach Nielson's eyes on me. He looked worried. I pretended to laugh at something, like I was feeling no pain. The last thing I wanted was for Coach to think I was an injury risk.

A moment later, Darius walked up behind me. "You mess with the bull and you get the horns, little man. There's plenty more where that came from," he said.

I refused to back down. "Bring it," I said.

And bring it he did. So did Javier, and Mike, and the rest of Darius's friends. For the next few hours, I was a marked man. Every time I touched the puck I ended up getting flattened. Sure, I scored a goal or two and handled the puck well. I definitely proved myself to be the fastest player on the ice, too. But I was getting knocked around like a ping-pong ball.

During the last game of the day, Coach had seen enough. Javier knocked me into the boards. His giant body smashed into me so hard that we had to replace one of the pieces of plastic. I slumped to the ground slowly before rising to my feet. Coach Nielson blew his whistle, stopping play. He skated over to me, yelling. "You've got to protect yourself, Miller! Skate with your head up, or you'll get killed out here."

"Yes, Coach," I said.

"Take a seat and catch your breath," Coach said, skating toward center ice.

I refused to quit. So I pumped my legs and skated toward him. Before the puck dropped I said, "I'm okay, Coach. I can stay in."

"I said take a seat, Miller! Nick, get in for Miller."

There was nothing I could do. So I made my way over to the bench. The tryouts ended a few minutes later.

I kept to myself in the locker room. I showered quickly and was dressed before everybody else. Fifteen minutes later, I was back on the ice. One by one, the guys also made their way out. Darius and his friends stood in a circle. They were apart from everyone else. They joked and laughed with each other. The rest of us looked on anxiously. Finally, Coach Nielson joined us on the ice.

I knew that I'd had a pretty good tryout. But Coach was looking more nervous every time I was hit. "Guys, this is the hardest part of being a coach. I really wish I could keep all of you, but I can't." He began handing out single sheets of paper. "I'm handing you a list of this year's team. If your name is on the list, meet here tomorrow at four. If not, thanks for coming out."

Coach Nielson didn't look me in the eyes as he handed me the list. I knew right then that I had been cut. I checked anyway, but the name Miller was nowhere to be found. I hung my head.

Darius skated past me on his way out, "Better luck next year, little man." He and Javier laughed as they left the building. I bit my lip to hold back the tears that wanted to pour out.

When everyone was gone I sat on the bench alone. Mom was waiting for me out front, but I just couldn't move. Coach Nielson sat down beside me. "You play just like your Dad, Wayne."

"Thank you," I said respectfully. "My father never got cut from a team, though, sir."

"Don't get down. You're a talented kid—maybe the most talented player out there. And you've got heart." He paused, "But Wayne . . ."

I cut him off, "I'm too small, right? Talent isn't enough."

"I'm afraid you're going to get hurt, son. You're only twelve. These guys are older than you—and much bigger. Hockey's a rough sport. You saw it today. You were getting killed out there."

"You took me out, Coach. I never took myself out. I scored twice and I'm the fastest guy out there. I can help this team win. I'm not scared of taking a hit."

Coach looked me right in the eyes when he said: "That's what I'm afraid of. Your Dad played the same way. Look what happened to him. And he was big, Wayne. I just—I can't put you out there right now."

I swallowed hard and got to my feet. "I guess I understand," I said. Then I shook his hand and left the building.

Darius and his idiot friends had ruined my chances. My big mouth had cost me big this time. It cost me a spot on the team.

CHAPTER FOUR

THE EQUIPMENT MANAGER

I squint as we make our way into the arena. My eyes are slowly adjusting to the bright lights. We begin to skate around in a circle. The fans are loud and excited for the season's opening game.

Most of the players try to ignore the crowd. Instead, they focus on their pre-game warm ups. John Simpson, a three-time All-Star, skates directly in front of me. I remember watching him on TV as a kid. He moves his head from side to side as he skates. He speeds up and then slows down. Having been here before, he seems completely calm.

I can't help but stare at the people in the stands. My eyes are everywhere, taking in a professional hockey game—from the ice. I begin looking for my parents. After a minute or two, I find them. They're both dressed from head to toe in Minnesota

Elk gear. They are parked ten rows up near center ice. They look excited. Dad gives me a fist pump when he notices me looking at him. Mom snaps a picture. I don't dare wave.

The guys spread out for some passing and shooting drills. At this point, our opponents are skating onto the ice. Loud boos fill the air. The Chicago Firestorm skate around and begin their warm-ups. Being a huge hockey fan, this is a strange moment for me. Many of the players on the ice were my idols growing up. Now I will be skating alongside them. It is both a weird and an amazing feeling.

I notice a television camera crew to my left. They're taping our warm-ups. A broadcaster is interviewing Coach Lewis near our bench. He is taking notes as Coach speaks. I wonder what notes, if any, he has written about me.

Alexi Kornikov skates up to me. He slaps me on the back with his stick. "You ready for big time?" he asks.

I nod my head. "I hope so," I tell him.

He reaches back and smashes the hardest slap shot I have ever seen. Amazingly, our goalie, Dave Furion, makes the save. Dave smacks the puck back to me. I reach back and take a quick one-timer. My shot is wide right and Furion doesn't even flinch.

I am embarrassed by my terrible shot. I race toward the puck near the right boards. With my legs pumping quickly, I show off my speed. I remember *all the hours I spent working on my skating.*

The drive home from tryouts was awful. Every word Mom said made me more upset. "You'll try again next year," she offered. Then she paused, adding, "You're bound to grow. And if you don't, that's okay too. You're smart and funny and creative. You can do all kinds of things." I knew this advice came from her heart, I just wished she would let me be.

As Mom talked, I stared out the window. I wanted to tell her that I wasn't giving up on hockey. Getting cut was a fluke. I didn't get cut because I was a bad player. I was cut because of Darius the Jerk Gray! I couldn't tell her this, though. If I did, I knew I would start crying. So we rode the rest of the way home in silence.

After we finished a quiet dinner, I went upstairs. Ricky called me, and I told him all about tryouts. He told me that I was lucky I got cut. Now I would only have to deal with Darius and his friends at school. I didn't feel lucky. I wanted to play hockey so badly. I would have gladly put up with Darius for the chance to play.

For the next hour, I listened to a Minnesota Elk game on the radio. When Dad knocked on my bedroom door, I flicked it off. I was in bed at this point, tossing my lucky puck into the air. My body ached from tryouts. Still, all I could think about was getting back on the ice.

"Feel like talking about it?" he asked as he slowly opened my door.

"Not really."

Dad sat down on the foot of my bed anyway. He looked up at me and smiled. "Coach Nielson called me. He said you played your heart out." He paused to wait for a response. When there wasn't one, he added, "I'm proud of you."

"I got cut, Dad, did Coach Nielson tell you *that*?"

"He did." Dad paused and then stared deep into my eyes. "Wayne, your Mom and I love you whether or not you play hockey. You know that, right?"

I nodded my head. "Mom already told me all of that stuff." I said. "I can be anything I want to be— I know. But I want to be a hockey player." I tossed my lucky puck onto the floor.

Dad reached down and picked it up, staring at it for a few seconds. "I know what it's like to have a dream." He took a deep breath, "You've got a long road to get there—a hard road. And your dream only dies the day you let it die. If you want today to be that day, that's okay."

"No way," I said. "I'm not quitting."

"Good," Dad smiled, "you're stubborn like your old man. Then don't worry. This is just a bump in the road. If you're serious about getting there, get ready for a lot more bumps. I came real close to my dream, Wayne. I just missed it." Dad smiled again,

"I'm happy with the way my life turned out. My point is that it's okay if things don't work out the way you plan them. Going for it, though, giving it everything you've got—that's what counts."

I sat up in bed, a few tears rolling down my cheeks. "I love hockey. I love it so much. I just wish I were bigger, like you. If I were . . ."

Dad reached over and wiped the tears away from my face. "You're not big. Crying about not being big isn't going to make you any bigger." Dad grabbed me by the shoulders. "What you've got is this little body, Wayne." He pointed to my chest, "and a big heart. Do the best you can with what you've got."

At this point, I stopped crying. "You're right," I said. I banged my chest with my fist. "This little guy is gonna make it to the NHL."

The next day at four o'clock I showed up at the middle school hockey rink. When I stepped into the locker room, my face turned bright red. Being there felt strange. Yesterday, we all tried out together. I had been cut. I was sure the guys were wondering what I was doing back today.

I took a deep breath before knocking on Coach's office door. He invited me in. To start, I explained that I understood his reasons for cutting me. I didn't agree with them, but I understood. There were no grudges and no hard feelings. I went on to tell him that I wasn't giving up my dream. Hockey was too important to me. I needed to be around the sport. I wasn't asking him for anything. I was offering something: my services as equipment manager.

At first, Coach wasn't sure if he liked the idea. He didn't want me to be frustrated the entire season long. "Are you sure you want to do this?" he asked.

"Absolutely," I said. "Hockey's in my blood. Being around the game can only make me better."

Coach was quiet for a moment. "Sit down," he said.

I sat down in the chair on the opposite side of his desk. "I'll do whatever you ask me to, Coach." I looked up at him with hopeful eyes.

"Don't ask me for playing time—even during practice. You won't get a jersey or a locker. No special privileges of any kind. You understand me?"

"Yes, Coach."

"You still interested?"

"Yes, no special privileges." I said. "I wouldn't want them. I just want to be around the game. I'll practice on my own time."

"Okay, Miller," he said, "then you're our equipment manager. Be here fifteen minutes before every practice. Get the goals set up, water bottles filled, and get the pucks and sticks out. Be dressed in skates and pads every day. That's just in case we need a body during practice—which we probably won't."

"Yes, sir," I smiled.

"You want to play in the NHL, right, Miller? I

can help you get there. Bring a notebook and a pen to practice—every day. Whatever you notice, I want you to write it down in that notebook. Then we'll talk about it. This will make you a better player."

"Thank you, Coach. I won't disappoint you. I'll stay out of the way, too." I shook his hand and started for the door. "I'll get that notebook."

"Miller," he shouted, before I left the room. "Don't quit on me. If you quit, don't even bother coming out for the team next year."

"Yes, sir," I said, leaving the room to set up for practice.

During the next few months I showed up to every practice and game. I was suited up twenty minutes before the guys arrived. I filled the water bottles, set up the goals, and did whatever else needed to be done. Occasionally, Coach had me set up cones on the ice for skating drills. Other times, he had me set up only one goal for defensive drills.

At first, Darius and his buddies really picked on me. I tried my best to ignore them, but sometimes that was impossible. There were more than a few fights between Darius and me. Coach usually had to step in and break us up. I was always thankful when he did.

Coach Nielson invited me to practice once in a while. Usually, it was when one of the guys didn't show up. I took advantage of every chance I got to step on the ice. Most of the time, I didn't play. I would sit on the sidelines with my pen and notebook. At first, I didn't really know what to write. I jotted down which players hit the hardest slap shots. I noted who was the fastest. I even ranked every player on the team in these areas. Coach was quick to point out that I was "missing the big picture." He ripped up my first few entries. "All the stats in the world don't make a great hockey player, Wayne. They sure as heck don't make a great team."

As the season continued, I started to understand what he meant. I started noticing little hockey details. I found that some guys went for the big check too often. When they missed, the entire team broke down defensively. I also found that most of our passes were at least a foot behind. When this happened, fast breaks became turnovers. Passing, I was realizing, was a key to good offense. When our team made three solid passes, we almost always got a shot on goal. When we worked together, we were ten times better. The same went for defense. When guys helped each other, scoring on us was impossible. I wrote these things down every day. After practice, I talked them over with Coach Nielson.

I liked taking notes on the game. But don't think that I didn't want to be out on the ice. I couldn't wait to put my new hockey knowledge to work. When I explained this to Coach, he helped me out. After some begging, he gave me a spare key to the rink. When practice ended, I was able to skate around until I could barely move. I found that when it came to speed, my size could be an advantage. Turning and changing directions was easier for a smaller player. Being low to the ground helped keep me balanced—especially when I turned. Finally, an advantage for the little guys!

CHAPTER FIVE

BIG BREAK

After warm-ups, we stand for the national anthem. We then listen as the starting lineups are announced. The laser light show at Elk Arena is incredible. I have certainly come a long way from pick-up games at Mickey's.

Finally, we are set to begin. Our starting line takes the ice. The crowd begins to pump in loud applause. Another NHL season is about to begin! I make my way to the end of the long bench and find a seat. My right arm hangs over the short barrier. I lean forward, stick in hand. I am ready to jump over and go to battle. My leg shakes up and down. I could not be more excited.

The ref skates out to the middle of the ice. A few words are exchanged between the starting centers. I wonder what they are saying to one another.

Suddenly, the two men are in a silent crouch, await-
ing the puck drop. I lean in closer, waiting for the
puck to hit the ice. The ref skates to within a few feet
of the two professionals. He holds the puck between
them, high in the air—then he drops it.

Mom always says that things happen for a reason. Honestly, I never believed her when she said this.
Then something very strange happened to me. Now I
think that Mom might have been right.

The day before my cafeteria run-in with Darius
Gray, Mom had bumped into Dr. Morris. Dr. Morris
had been my doctor since I was a baby. He and Mom
were chatting while in line at the supermarket. He men-
tioned that the flu was going around. Anyway, Mom
got worried and made me an appointment for the next
day. I remember being annoyed that I had to get a flu
shot. As it turned out, that flu shot saved my season.

Dr. Morris didn't bump into enough people that
fall. By the time winter came around, everybody had
the flu. Ricky got it so bad that he was in bed for two
weeks. Mr. Weathers, who always gave me a hard time,
got it too. So did Principal Wilson and two of my
other teachers.

Meanwhile, led by Darius Gray, the middle
school hockey team was 6 and 5. I was on the sidelines, with my notebook in hand. There were just three
games left in the season. Making the playoffs was
going to be tough. The guys would have to win two

of their last three games. They felt as if they had a really good chance, until the flu. It hit the team hard.

The big game against Plymouth Middle School was to be Tuesday night. Coach Nielson scheduled practice at four o'clock on Monday afternoon. As usual, I was there early, setting up. Coach told me to arrange the cones for skating drills. Before the guys arrived, I had everything ready. I even got to skate through the course myself a few times.

I glanced around the rink just before practice started. Something was off. The rink was virtually empty. There were supposed to be eighteen players on the team. With the clock reading just three minutes before four, only twelve had shown up. This was an all-time low for practice attendance. Coach Nielson looked worried. He sat in his office talking on the phone. All the while, he chewed on his fingernails.

The team had started to lose players to the flu last week. They were down to just fifteen guys for last Thursday's game. It appeared as though a few more had gone down since then. By 4:15, there were thirteen players huddled near center ice. Everyone was asking nervous questions. Had anyone heard from Darius? Who else was sick? When were they coming back? How were they going to compete against Plymouth?

I was sitting on the sidelines. I leaned up in my seat as Coach skated onto the ice. With fifteen players, the roster had been very thin last week. With only thirteen, I wasn't sure the guys could compete against Plymouth. If there was ever a time that this team needed me, it was then. My skates were on. My stick was close. My heart was racing.

"Okay, fellas, calm down!" Coach yelled. The guys stopped talking and formed a tight circle around Coach. "How's everybody feeling?" He looked around at each player. "Anybody have a scratchy throat, feeling hot, anything like that?"

The guys shook their heads, one by one. "Good, then we've got thirteen healthy guys for tomorrow's game." Coach said. "Everybody in this town seems to have gotten the flu. Darius's got it, Craig's got it. I just spoke to Brock's Mom—he's got it too. Mike, Jesse, and Nick are getting better. They'll be out for tomorrow's game, though." Coach cleared his throat. "Right now, we need to be a team more than ever." He turned around and faced me. "Wayne, drop your notebook and get over here."

He didn't have to ask me twice. Before he finished his sentence, I was skating toward the team. I assumed that I would be practicing today. Having an extra body out there would be a big help.

It turned out that Coach was looking for more than a body. Very matter-of-factly, he said, "Wayne's on the team for the rest of the year. You've all played with him. He hustles, he's quick, and he's got heart. Plus, he got a flu shot. Welcome aboard, Miller—we're glad to have you." I smiled. I'd gotten my big break.

Now I just had to take advantage of it.

The reaction I got from the guys was mixed. I heard a few guys clap and a few others sigh. I even heard a "not Miller" comment.

"Okay, guys, line up for some skating. Wayne, come over here," Coach Nielson blew his whistle. I skated over to him. The rest of the team formed a line behind the cones. He spoke to me in a loud voice, "You earned this. Don't let anybody tell you different."

"Yes, sir," I said.

"Now get in line!"

I skated over to the rest of the team. Coach drifted toward the opposite end of the cones course. The cones were set up about ten feet apart from one another. This meant that there was no chance of reaching full speed. This drill was all about quickness. At the end of the course, Coach dropped a puck. It was about fifteen feet from the goal. When a player reached the puck, he was supposed to shoot it in. Coach held a stopwatch in his hand and timed us. If you knocked over a cone, five seconds were added to your time. If you missed the shot, ten seconds.

I was last in line. I waited for my turn as each player finished. With two guys left, I started getting antsy. I couldn't help but imagine myself ripping through the course. Other thoughts ran through my brain: *Wait until the guys see my speed. They'll have no choice but to accept me as a teammate then.*

For now, I had to deal with some doubters. "Way to sneak your way onto the team, Miller. You'll screw this up for sure." Javier Cervantes spoke into my ear. He was the last of Darius's friends not to get the flu. Before I could think about what he'd said, Javier finished his run.

"Miller, you're up," Coach shouted. Then he blew his whistle and clicked his stopwatch.

I took off, tearing through the course at a record pace. My skates felt as if they were a part of my feet. I was as light as a feather, and as smooth as the ice I glided on. With five cones behind me, I was staring down a perfect run. I was confident that my time would be the best of the day.

With just two cones left, I started focusing on the puck. I planned on shooting while skating—never slowing down. I'd done this before. Although it wasn't easy, I was sure I could do it. The looks of shock on the faces of my teammates would tell the story. The equipment manager was about to have the best run of the day!

I pumped my legs and sped toward the final cone. Then I changed directions to angle myself for a shot on goal. I could tell I was moving fast. When I turned to face the goal I had just about reached the puck. I started my backswing. Lifting my stick into the air made me lose my balance. Instead of slowing to a stop, I tried to shoot while falling. This was a bad idea. When I swung at the puck, I never touched it.

My stick hit the ice, followed by my body.

Lying on the ice, I heard Coach yell, "You're out of control, Miller."

I hung my head. I had wasted an opportunity.

I woke up the next morning with a new attitude. It was hard, but I put my big spill behind me. That night, we would be playing against Plymouth—my first game of the season. With only fourteen players, I would be seeing plenty of ice time. This thought excited me. Unfortunately, I was sure my teammates had little confidence in me. I had a lot to prove against Plymouth and I knew it.

The game started with me on the bench. I was nervous. Still, being a part of the team was a great feeling. Our first line was giving Plymouth all they could handle early on. I found myself cheering louder than ever now that I was in uniform.

At six minutes into the first period, the puck was slapped down the boards. We quickly changed lines. Coach put me in at right wing. I skated onto the ice with a smile on my face. I moved around like crazy during the next few minutes. I never got near the puck, though.

I did land a solid check on a Plymouth forward. He was coming into our zone on the break. I stopped him cold. For a little guy, my check packed a mean punch. Overall, it was a good start to my season—even though it was a late start.

Coach slapped my helmet as I made my way

back onto the bench. "Way to play defense, Miller." His comment was music to my ears.

I sat down on the bench and waited for my next chance to play. I didn't have to wait long. A few minutes later, I was back out there. This time, I was really going to impress Coach Nielson. I skated into position on the right side of the ice. Another forward was skating right at me with the puck. I went for a stick poke, but missed by a long shot. He made a nice move, switching hands and faking me out of my skates.

Oh, no, I thought. *I just gave them a fast break!* I tried to recover, but it was too late. They made a few quick passes that led to an easy goal. My mistake had cost us a goal. It was 1-0 Plymouth.

When I got to the bench, a couple of guys were talking about my mistake. Coach Nielson saw that I was upset. He made his way over to me. "Keep your head up!" He yelled. "If you lose your confidence, you can't help this team. Make up for it on your next shift. Remember what we talked about—let the game come to you." This was exactly what I needed to hear. I knew this game. I was simply trying too hard. Forcing things never made for good hockey.

When I came back in at the end of the second, I was a different player. I was no longer trying to force a big play. Instead, I was focused on my part of the ice. I drifted backwards when my opponent's pushed up. My defense forced Plymouth to make extra passes to cross into our zone.

With four minutes left in the period, I got my first big chance. I waited for their right wing to enter my zone. On the last play, he'd waited until he reached the blue line to make a pass. When he did pass, it was back across the ice to his center. He skated toward the blue line again. I got ready to pounce. Sure enough, he decided to pass back to the middle again. I took off the moment the puck left his stick.

I was able to cut off the pass and make a break for the goal. Next, I made a nice crossover move on their center. I left him in the dust. Their defensemen had been pushing up, so they had no chance to recover. They were drifting backwards when I was reaching top speed. I flew past them like a flash of lightning.

Before I knew it, I was fifteen feet from the goal. The goalie flinched left on my fake. I quickly reacted, moving the puck to my backhand. Then I poked one in from five feet out. Goal! Tie score!

Scoring that goal was the greatest feeling I had ever felt on the ice. I had never worked so hard for an opportunity. My teammates circled me in celebration. Even Javier Cervantes gave me a chest bump. For the first time, I was no longer the equipment manager. I was a part of the team.

With my confidence soaring, I scored again three plays later. I was the star of the game as we beat Plymouth 3-1. We were still alive in the playoff hunt.

CHAPTER SIX

TEAMMATES

When I woke up this morning, I felt confident. I was sure that I was ready for the speed and power of an NHL game. Sitting just a few feet from the action, I'm seeing things differently. These guys are faster than anything I imagined. Plus, they all seem to be built like trucks. I'm starting to wonder if my speed will even be a factor. This thought scares me for a second. I'm the smallest guy on either team. If I'm not the fastest guy out there, then where's my edge?

In the middle of this thought, Coach Lewis yells over to me. "Miller, get in there!"

The puck is smacked along the boards. I jump out of my seat with my heart beating through my chest. A second later, I am playing in an NHL game. The moment my skates touch the ice, my doubts dis-

appear. Everything actually feels okay. Yes, I do belong here. I am at home on the ice.

I keep my eye on the puck as I drift back on defense. It is being passed around quickly. The whooshing sound it makes is unmistakable. Each whoosh is followed by a smack. It's the sound of a perfect pass. This sound is music to my ears. Dad used to say that only true hockey players could appreciate the noises of the game. These noises have never been clearer to me.

I don't dare push up into the Firestorm's zone. I'm waiting for the rest of my line to get into position. Finally, we're set. I skate forward on the attack, pressuring the defense. Unlike high school or college, these defensemen are unaffected by my pressure. Still, I keep coming. I imagine that I look fast to them. I'm sure that my speed is not what they notice right now, though. More likely, they notice that I am young, overmatched—and tiny.

The puck moves around behind the Firestorm's goal. Our right wing goes after it. He lays a nice check on a Firestorm defender. The puck is smacked around the boards and into our zone. I drift back again. Then I slow to a stop. I am alone on the right side of center ice. For the moment, I appear to be open. Before I even realize this, a sharp pass comes toward me. I wait for it. Then I look up the ice, ready to make a run.

The puck makes contact with my stick. At that

exact moment, a blur of red and black smashes into me. He leads with his shoulder and blasts me back into the boards. I slump to my knees. The fans are oohing and aahing behind me. Not only do I lose the puck, but my stick as well.

Our defense grabs the loose puck. We smack it back down the boards. My body is in shock. That was the hardest hit I have ever taken. I grab my stick and skate back to the bench for a line change.

Everything changed for me after the Plymouth game. I was no longer the equipment manager. The guys treated me differently. So did Coach Nielson. I was part of the team now. I had earned everyone's respect.

Strangely, I found myself spending a lot of time with Javier. We had been at odds with each other early on in the year. The eighth grader was actually a good guy, though. He was quick with an apology and I was just as quick to forgive him. He had actually felt bad for me when Darius poured food on my head in the cafeteria. He apologized for not stepping in and helping me. Sure, he was bigger and stronger than Darius. But standing up to the bully was a hard thing to do. I understood this.

Being a part of the team was great. Something was happening to me on the ice that was even better. Every day my game was taking a giant leap. My skating, my passing, my shooting—everything was improving. I was a quiet leader during practice, too. I gave an all-out effort on every play. My hustle pushed my teammates to work harder.

By the following week, our roster started to fill in again. A few more guys came back from their battles with the flu. Darius was still sick, though. The seventeen of us who remained were really starting to gel. We were coming together in a way we hadn't with Darius on the ice. There was no more fear of looking stupid. Nobody was worried about Darius yelling when he didn't touch the puck. In his absence, we began to play as a team. The results were amazing. We won the next two games after beating Plymouth—outscoring our opponents 11-2! In doing so, we qualified for the playoffs.

Darius Gray joined us during our last practice before the big game. As quickly as we'd come together, we fell apart. Darius was not happy to see that I was on the roster. That much was for sure. He was really nasty to me. Of course, my game fell to pieces. I was totally rattled by Darius. Once again, I was trying too hard to make plays. I became too aggressive, leaving my zone and taking wild shots. I left practice feeling awful. I couldn't play like that during tomorrow's game.

Darius was right there to point out my shortcomings. He pointed out the shortcomings of our teammates as well. He was *so* mean that many players turned into statues on the ice. They didn't want to be called out by Darius. Guys who were making plays a few days earlier, disappeared. The moment they touched the puck, they would be searching for Darius. Once they found him, they would force a pass in to him. Our team was falling apart at the seams.

Ricky and I hung out at the arcade that night. I talked to him about the way the team was playing with Darius back. Ricky could tell that I was really worried about our upcoming game. He said that there was probably nothing I could do. "Just wait until next year when Darius is off to high school. Don't worry about this year."

That was impossible. I was too competitive. I told Ricky that we were going to change his nickname. "Forget Quick Rick, we should call you Scared Stiff Rick!" He laughed, and then punched me in the arm.

We ate some ice cream and played video games for the next hour. Ricky set a record on the mini basketball pop-a-shot machine. He was unbelievable at that game. I told him that he should go out for the basketball team next year. He was seriously thinking about it. Ricky could shoot the lights out. Plus, while I stayed the same height year after year, Ricky grew like a weed.

We were in the middle of our fifth game when Javier came over to us. He was with a few girls. When Ricky saw them, his grip tightened on the basketball. He tried to stand behind me. It probably looked funny—Ricky hiding behind me. I was only as tall as his shoulders.

Javier called out, "What's happening, Wayne?" He slapped my hand and I introduced Javier to Ricky. My best friend was shocked when the eighth grader bumped knuckles with him. The girls Javier walked in with were also eighth graders. These two beauties were *way* out of our league. Javier was about to introduce us. But then Darius entered the room. He started walking toward us. I knew right away that this was going to be trouble.

Darius came toward me like he was about to check me into the boards. Only there weren't any boards. "Look who it is, our team mascot and his nerdy friend." Darius laughed loudly at his joke. "You guys are the stupidest looking pair I've ever seen." He walked up to Ricky. "This guy's as tall as house and as skinny as a stick." Then he came up to me. "I can barely even see this little geek. You look like an elf, Miller."

Ricky whispered to me right away, "Let's go, Wayne."

"Hey, Darius," I said, playing off his comment. "Always good to see you, buddy." After I made my sarcastic comment, I turned around and pretended Darius wasn't there.

"I'm not your buddy," he said under his breath.

I barely heard him. I had already turned my back and started talking to Javier. "Check this out, Javy," I said. I pulled a small bag from my pocket. "I got new laces for my skates—blue and white."

"Team colors," Javier said. "You know what I thought would be cool? If we all cut our hair like—"

Darius cut Javier off. He put his hand on the big defensemen's shoulder. "We? Why are you saying "we" to this loser? He's not one of us. He's the equipment manager. If we all didn't get sick, he'd still be filling our water bottles. Think about it." Darius got in my face. "Don't think I'm going to treat you any different. You weaseled your way onto the team, Miller."

His comment hurt my feelings at first. Then I realized something: "Since you got sick, we've won three games in a row. Think about that." After I said these words I turned my back on Darius again.

When I wasn't looking, Darius came running at me. I didn't see him coming until the last second. Then I closed my eyes, hoping that no bones would break. I was going to be smashed into the pop-a-shot machine. Just before Darius reached me, Javier stepped in front of him. He stopped him in his tracks and knocked him to the ground.

"What the heck are you doing, Javier?" Darius screamed. Then he pushed Javier, before storming out of the arcade. "Forget you—you traitor!"

I let out a deep and long sigh of relief. Then I slapped Javier on the back. If not for him blocking Darius, I would have been leveled.

My emotions changed faster than an NHL slap-shot. I quickly began to worry about our big game the next day. Like it or not, Darius was the best player on our team. He represented our best chance of winning. This fight was not a good thing.

The following afternoon was the first playoff game. We were facing Sandburg Middle School. They had won the section last year. Sandburg finished the regular season with the same record as we did.

I started that game on the bench. Darius took back his position on the first line. From the start of that game, we weren't playing as a team. Everyone was standing around watching Darius. He was an incredible player—probably the best on the ice. But he hogged the puck. He never passed. Playing one on five wasn't going to result in a win. Even with the best player, we were totally outmatched.

Within a few minutes, Sandburg scored their first goal. I entered the game just after that. I skated after loose pucks and hustled back to play defense. Meanwhile, Darius sat on the bench and pouted. My line gave Sandburg all they could handle for the next ten minutes. Then I skated to the bench. I sat down a few seats away from Darius.

The first period ended with us trailing by one. Coach put Darius's line in to start the second. Once again, our offense struggled when our star player was on the ice. He managed to get one shot on goal, but his defense was terrible. One minute into the period,

Sandburg struck again and took a 2-0 lead.

Coach immediately called a timeout. "Let's start playing like a team out there. Make the extra pass, help each other on defense. Come on, guys!" He looked over at Darius. "We have to play together." Coach scratched his head, before saying, "Wayne, get in at left wing. Darius, stay in with the second line." He looked at both of us. It was obvious that he felt the tension between us. "You don't have to be best friends, but be teammates!"

I looked over at Darius, who rolled his eyes at me. Then he bumped into me as we skated onto the ice. "Stay out of my way."

So much for being teammates, I thought.

Right from the face-off, Coach Nielson's experiment looked like a disaster. Darius continued to hog the puck. He made sure to never even look in my direction. It seemed like nothing could bring us together.

While Darius was skating near center ice, I trailed him. My hope was that he would drop the puck back to me. This would give me a clear shot on goal. So far, I had no such luck. I skated fifteen feet behind him. Suddenly, I noticed a defensive player charging him. I could tell that Darius didn't see him coming. When I saw the defender break, I broke. I had to stop him. If Darius were blindsided, he would lose the puck. Then Sandburg would have another fast break. I knew that if we went down by three goals, the game would be over. Although part of me wanted to see Darius get leveled, I knew what I had to do.

Just before the defensive player reached Darius, I lunged toward him. I gave up my body for my teammate. My smallish frame collided with the defensive player's body. We tumbled to the ground. Darius turned around just in time to see the collision. He took advantage of the open ice. He skated past a slower defender, before firing a slap shot that landed in the back of the net.

I was lying on the ice when I saw the goal go in. I raised my fist high into the air. Turning to face me, Darius skated back from the goal. He reached out his hand and helped me to my feet. "Thanks, Wayne."

"We're teammates, Darius. You don't have to thank me."

"Thanks anyway." Darius shook my hand. "Let's win this!" he said. That was as close as I would ever get to an apology from Darius. I smiled, knowing that his days of pushing me around were over.

The rest of the game was a blur of excitement. Trailing Sandburg by a goal, Darius and I went on the offensive. Coach was right, we *were* a dynamic duo. My speed and his big shot were a deadly combination. We scored five more times and went on to win by a final of 6-3.

The next game was the final. We played a team that was ranked in the state. They were great at every position. Not surprisingly, we lost. But we played well.

We took the game into overtime before falling 1-0.

Darius moved to California the next year. That was the last game I would ever have to play with him.

CHAPTER SEVEN

TIME FLIES

I am back on the bench. The final seconds of the first period tick away. After taking that hard hit, I'm a little dizzy. Everything is spinning—I feel like a piece of clothing in the washing machine.

The first period comes to an end. Alexi Kornikov sits to my right on the bench. "You took big hit, huh?"

"I'm all right," I say, rolling my neck so that it cracks. "I never saw that guy coming."

"Sometimes big hit wake you up!" he says.

I smile at him. He jumps over the boards with the rest of the first line. We are about to begin the second period. "I'm up now!" I call out, as he moves into position at left wing.

The second period is very defensive, just like the first. Neither team is getting clean shots off. "Let them make the mistake," is the advice Dad had always given me. "At some point, even the best players make mental errors. It's only a matter of time." I kept this thought in the back of my head.

Twelve minutes are left in the second when the whistle blows. We are called for a penalty. It's hooking on John Simpson. He yells at the ref as if he's innocent. Simpson never goes down without a fight. Coach calls over his penalty-killing line from the bench. Before he sends them in, he pulls out Nick Brolefski. Then he looks over at me and yells, "Miller, get in at right wing. Show us some speed, kid." I am shocked that I have been called in with this line.

For two minutes, we will only have four players on the ice. This is a huge opportunity for our opponents. It is also a big responsibility for me. Coach Lewis thinks that my speed will be useful. I have to prove him right. My job is to be everywhere all at once.

When I get out on the ice, Five Firestorm players come at us on the attack. They spread out in our zone. Their one-man advantage always leaves someone open. The first pass is made into the corner. I am focused on the puck. Our right defenseman checks a Firestorm forward. We gain possession of the puck. Our forward hammers one along the boards. That play will buy about fifteen seconds. Then they'll be back on the attack.

Before I can catch my breath, they're coming

again. Their center makes a quick pass to the wing. I stand tall (well, as tall as I can) to face him. He fakes a pass back to center. I don't flinch. I hold my ground. He fires a pass back to a trailing defenseman. I attack. The defenseman sees me coming. He spins and tries to pass back to the right wing. I intercept his pass and begin skating toward the goal. The crowd gets loud! They are about to see a one-on-one showdown with the goalie.

I played on the hockey team as a seventh grader. That season was a lot of fun for me. Off the ice, something amazing was happening to me. I was growing! When I measured myself against my bedroom wall I saw that I had grown three inches! That was the most I had ever grown in one year.

By the time eighth grade came around, I was four foot nine. I was no giant, but I wasn't the shortest kid in school either. It helped that I was older than most of the kids. Either way, I wasn't the shortest, and it felt great.

While I barely grew, Ricky shot up like a weed. This helped him to be a star on the basketball court. My best friend now stood over six feet tall. He towered over me by more than a foot. I joked around with him sometimes about being so tall. I called him Godzilla.

I was elected captain of the hockey team during eighth grade. I had a great season, too. I earned the MVP award and was an assist-machine. My twenty-six.assists led the entire league! The guy who finished second had only twelve. I had really found my comfort zone on the ice. I owed a lot of that to Coach Nielson.

It was hard for me to leave Coach at the end of middle school. I knew that the competition was tougher in high school. I wondered how I would handle it without him. Coach taught me so much about the game. "Great teams don't have twenty guys with great slap shots. They don't have twenty guys who can check, either. Great teams have guys who use their unique strengths."

Thanks to Coach Nielson, I was well aware of my strengths. I was a speedy skater, a deadly passer, and a great defensive player. I planned on building on these skills in high school.

I made the junior varsity team as a freshman. This was a pretty big deal because only one other freshman made it. During eighth grade, I had felt like the king of middle school. I had tons of friends and I was captain of the hockey team. When I got to high school, all of that changed. The guys on my team had facial hair. They drove their cars to practice. Most of them had girlfriends, too. I had never shaved. I was two years away from getting my license. Plus, I'd only been on one date.

Hanging out with the guys on the team was pretty much all I did. Javier was a junior, which helped a lot. He was bigger than ever. Having Javy watching my back made high school easier. In terms of grades, I was doing great. My first semester of high school was the first time I'd earned a 4.0!

When sophomore year began, I was much more comfortable. I grew another inch and easily made the varsity team. I played amazing hockey during tryouts. We had a good team that year. I managed to make my way onto the first line. Being on the starting line was something I was proud of. At fifteen, I stood at five foot three. Once again, I was the smallest guy on the team. At that point, though, I was used to it. I rarely felt bad about being short anymore. When I did, I would think back to what my father had told me: "What you've got is this little body, Wayne. And a big heart. Do the best you can with what you've got." From that day on, I had.

We reached the sectional finals that year. We lost, though. Roosevelt killed us, 6-0. I played terribly during that final contest. This made me work twice as hard on my game that summer.

All I did during July and August was work out. I was a high school hockey player trying to get a college scholarship. I knew it was all about my junior and senior seasons. The coming season was my first chance to show college scouts I could play. Unfortunately, I had a big strike against me—my size. Nobody wanted to give a scholarship to a guy as small as me. If I had any chance at earning a free ride, my game had to take off.

Many of my teammates joined the local gym that summer. Not me, though. I worked out the old-fashioned way. I ran ten miles every morning when I woke up. Then, at night, I went down to Mickey's. Once there, I scrimmaged with the older men. They would play in shifts, but I never left the ice. This was how I pushed myself to the limit. I even got the chance to play alongside my Dad that summer. Although he was slow, he still showed some flashes of greatness. I learned a lot from playing with him.

The routine I put myself through got me in the best shape of my life. And I did all of it without protein shakes and lifting. My strategy was different from most kids my age. Coach Nielson had taught me to play to my strengths. I was never going to be big, no matter how many shakes I drank. So I focused my energy on making myself fast. My goal was to be the fastest hockey player on earth. Super speed was my best chance of impressing scouts and coaches. I had to be the fastest guy they'd ever seen—because I would definitely be one of the smallest.

Our team was stacked during my junior year. *The Post*, our local paper, picked us to win the section. There was an article about us a week before the season started. The headline read, "Riding Little Wayne." It was all about me. According to the paper, I was going to make or break the season. This definitely put some pressure on me. I was proud of it. I cut it out and hung it on my wall. Little Wayne was the key to success on a team filled with talented players. That thought made me smile, even though they called me Little Wayne—a nickname I had never been able to get rid of.

Early on, the paper's prediction looked to be right on target. We won our first five games that season. I was playing better than ever. My summer workout program allowed me to keep skating while other players tired. My size was less of a factor now. I had super speed and was hard to hit. Players trying to check me often missed altogether. I even heard one coach telling his guys *not* to check me. "Just keep him in front of you," he yelled.

By mid-December, our mailbox was filled every day. Coaches from around the country were asking me to visit their schools. I was starting to get excited about the possibilities. If I continued improving, I was going to be playing Division I hockey.

Of course, there was only school I really wanted to attend. That was Minnesota College. The Silver Snakes had one of the most respected hockey programs in the country. Growing up, I had always been a fan. To me, the Snakes were the best when it came to college hockey.

In the middle of that season, I got a letter from Minnesota College. Assistant coach Pete Mitchum had taken notice of me. He said that the Minnesota College coaches would be keeping an eye on me. I had a chance to be a Silver Snake! I couldn't have been more excited.

Scouts attended nearly every game I played that season. We finished with a record of 12 and 2. That matched the best record our high school ever had. We barely lost the section to Wayzata High School in a 2-1 heartbreaker. I scored our lone goal, but it wasn't enough. Losing was disappointing. Still, most of the guys on our squad would be seniors next year. I was sure we would have a chance to win the entire thing then.

The first game of our senior season was against Copper River High School. They were well known for playing rough. They had huge players who were not very skilled. They rarely had a winning record. Playing them was always a tough game, though.

I got off to a great start by scoring a quick goal. That gave us a 1-0 lead against a team that had a hard time scoring. We took off from there, scoring twice more in the second period. In the third period, things got physical. Bodies were flying all over the place. With seven minutes remaining, I skated onto the ice for a line change. I had no idea that my life was about to change.

Everything seemed to happen in slow motion. I skated near the right boards, waiting for their offense to push up. Our left wing pressured the puck. His pressure caused a bad pass. I saw the loose puck and took off. My legs pumped and my skates pushed hard off the ice. I chased down that puck with everything I had. That was the only way I knew how to play hockey.

The puck was being kicked around near the boards. I stopped sharply once I reached it. My back was to their goal. I joined an opposing player who was trying to kick the puck. I couldn't smack it with my stick because I was being hooked. The defender was close enough for me to hear him grunting. I fought him off, even though he was stronger than me. Finally, I was able to get my skate blade on the puck. I kicked it into the middle of the ice like a soccer player.

As I was following through with my kick, I noticed a second defenseman. He was coming right at me. Then he tripped and fell. There was no time to get out of his way. His body was crashing toward me really fast. There was nothing I could do but wait for impact. My left leg was high in the air at this point. It was the only thing that broke his fall. His body landed awkwardly. I fell to the ground with him on top of me. The full weight of his 200-pound frame crashed down on my leg. I watched as it bent back in a strange way.

Right away, I screamed, "My leg! My leg!" A sharp pain shot through my body. I flipped around on the ice in pain. Coach raced out and helped carry me to the sidelines. The pain in my left leg was unbearable. Five minutes later, I was placed in an ambulance.

I arrived at the emergency room in terrible pain.

Things were about to get even worse, though. The doctors didn't wait long to deliver some awful news. My leg had been badly broken. My season was over. My leg might never be the same again. Disaster had struck.

Mom and Dad had both been at the game. They looked as terrified as I did when they got to the hospital. The doctor was casting my leg when Mom walked over to me. She squeezed my hand and looked into my eyes. Her soft kiss on my head did nothing to ease my pain, or hers.

With tears in his eyes, Dad stared over at my leg. He paced around the room in large circles. He wouldn't look into my eyes. Somehow, I knew he couldn't bear to. This injury was too similar to the one he had suffered. He knew the pain I was feeling— and I don't mean the pain in my leg. He had already been through this once. Back then, it was his leg that was broken. Back then, his dream had been crushed. In a sad twist of fate, the same thing had happened to his only son. It didn't seem fair.

It was hard to sleep in the hospital that night. My leg was wrapped in a giant cast and my heart was broken. I stared out the window at a newly fallen snow. Hours later, I watched the sun rise. When it did, I met another doctor. He told me that I would be in this cast for three months. Then I would begin my long recovery process. He also warned me that my leg might never be the same.

I couldn't help but replay that collision in my head. Why didn't I move out of the way? Why did I go after that puck? Why was I kicking it? There were no answers to these questions. There was only a dark hospital room and a broken leg.

When I listened closely, I could hear it—the silence of a broken dream.

CHAPTER EIGHT

A LONG ROAD

I am skating toward the goal with the puck. I am about to meet face to face with an NHL goalie. George Olen is one of the best in the business. Sneaking one past him is going to be tough. I start to make my move about fifteen feet out. First, I shift the puck over to my front side. Then I fake a slap shot. Olen flinches—I have an opening on his right! I quickly switch the puck over to my backhand. With a flick of my wrist, I dump one over his right shoulder.

I am five feet from him when the puck leaves my stick. My shot is on line. It's heading toward the upper left-hand corner. I wait for the flashing red lights to come on above the goal. Olen shifts his body. Somehow, the puck nicks the top of his shoulder. It slides over the top of the goal.

I try not to look disappointed or surprised. I

quickly skate to the back of the goal. I want that loose puck. When I arrive, though, a defender is there to meet me. He punishes me with a big hit. In the meantime, he grabs the puck and starts a fast break. I catch up to him at center ice. I don't dare try for the steal. Instead, I settle back into a good position to defend.

Thirty seconds are left on the Firestorm power play. We need to make one last stand. Sure enough, the Firestorm spread out in our zone again. They begin passing the puck around quickly. Without warning, their center makes a run. He skates past our left wing. A perfect pass hits him in stride. He reaches back and one-times a laser on goal.

The crowd is on their feet. Our goalie, Dave Furion, makes an incredible kick save. He extends his legs into a full split. What a save! Furion controls the puck. Standing up, he smacks it along the boards. The penalty is over. The crowd goes nuts!

I am exhausted. I skate over to the bench for a line change. A few of my teammates slap my helmet. This is a sign of respect.

I left the hospital two days after breaking my leg. It was early November, and winter was just around the corner. I spoke to Dr. Davis for an hour before leaving. He told me that my cast would likely come off in February. At that point I could *begin* my rehab. I was anxious to get that process started. I wasn't quitting—not by a long shot. I needed to get back to 100 percent by next August. This was nine months away. Then I could try to walk onto a college hockey team in the fall. I confessed this dream to Dr. Davis.

He was very supportive. He was also up front with me about my break. I had broken my femur. The femur is the largest bone in the human body. It is also a bone that takes time to heal—lots of time. The doctor warned me not to rush it. It would be a while before I could walk again. Even after my cast was removed! There was no timetable for regaining my full strength. "Many people who break their femur are never the same again." Dr. Davis got no joy from telling me this. He felt that he had to prepare me, though. There was a possibility that I would never play hockey again.

The first day back at school was strange. People were approaching me all day long. They came up and told me how sorry they were for me. Their sympathy actually made me feel worse. Still, I forced myself to smile at them. I told everyone I spoke to the same thing: "I'll be back out on the ice soon enough."

By the end of that day I wanted to crawl into a dark hole. A week ago, my life seemed perfect. I was a senior in high school. I was about to turn eighteen. Now, all the plans I'd been making had fallen apart. How would I ever make the NHL when I could barely get to hockey practice?

Watching the guys practice didn't feel real. I

kept waiting for my leg to feel better. Sitting on the sidelines reminded me of my days as equipment manager. Things were different now. I no longer felt pressure to prove myself. I had already been down that road. That feeling was replaced by a different feeling—helplessness. There was nothing I could do to help my leg heal. It drove me crazy.

With each passing day, my chances of playing in the NHL lessened. Hockey scholarships were being awarded. But letters from coaches stopped coming my way. One year ago, hundreds of colleges were interested in me. By January, the word of my injury had spread. Breaking my leg ended my chances for a college hockey scholarship.

My cast came off on February 15, three months after my injury. The hockey season was over at this point. I woke up whistling that morning. It was going to be a great day! My leg was about to be released from jail.

It took ten seconds for my cast to be cut off. When I saw my leg, my jaw dropped. It was pale and skinny. I could barely move it. It smelled disgusting. All muscle mass in the leg was gone. I didn't recognize this "thing" the doctor insisted was my leg.

Getting down from the table wasn't easy. I nearly fell to the ground. I glanced down at my leg—totally confused. Then I poked it with my finger. The leg was still there, but it had no strength. I had barely any feeling down there. The strange thing was that it didn't hurt—but it didn't work right either. A few tears welled up in my eyes. With Mom at my side, I swallowed hard to avoid crying. It was then that I realized how much work I had ahead of me. I left the hospital hobbling around on crutches. Cast or no cast, my leg was still in bad shape.

I got a letter a few weeks later that cheered me up. It was from Minnesota College. No, they didn't ask me to play hockey for them. I had been accepted to attend the college as a student, though. There was no scholarship offer. No mention of hockey at all. I accepted their offer the next day. I would be attending school in Minneapolis next fall.

I wasn't giving up on my hockey career. Since I was a kid, my plan was to play hockey at Minnesota College. Even though I was hurt, that was *still* my plan. I was starting to understand what Dad had told me a long time ago: "Your dream only dies the day you let it die." I wasn't ready to let it die yet. I planned on attending the open tryouts for the hockey team. There were two spots available for walk-ons. I planned on taking one of them. First, I needed to make a fast recovery. Tryouts were on August 10.

I started working with a physical trainer five days a week. Every morning before school, my alarm would ring at four thirty. I would start my one-mile walk to the hospital at five. My trainer suggested that I walk slowly the whole way. I did exactly what he told me. Every day my walk got easier.

At the training center we would do strength-building exercises. My leg improved a lot. Everything was happening very slowly, though. Each time I looked at the calendar, I panicked. I wondered if my leg would be strong enough for tryouts. We were creeping closer to August 10.

I graduated from high school with honors at the end of June. My final grade point average was a 3.7. This made me the fifteenth-ranked graduating senior. I planned on majoring in sports medicine that fall in Minneapolis. In rehabbing from my injury, I had become interested in this career. I worked hard on my leg and took mental notes on my treatment. For the first time, I was passionate about something besides hockey.

By the end of June, I was riding my bike five miles a day. My leg felt strong. It was hard to tell if I was ready to skate, though. I wouldn't know that until I got out on the ice and tested it. Finally, a month before hockey tryouts, my trainer gave me permission skate. I had made it all the way back! I no longer walked with a limp. I found myself forgetting that my leg had been injured. It had been eight months since I was lying on that ice in pain. I had worked as hard as I possibly could to get back. There was one thing left to do: play hockey.

The following Saturday morning was an exciting day. I planned on returning to the ice. From my days as equipment manager, I still had the key to the middle school rink. I drove over in Dad's truck. Then I flicked on the lights and opened the door. Nobody was there. I put on my skates and tied the laces tightly. It felt great to put on those skates again. Next, I put on pads. I wanted this to experience to be similar to a real game. Finally, I went out onto the ice. It was really weird to be skating again.

I took a slow lap around the rink. During that lap, I couldn't help but think about my leg. I couldn't shake this feeling of fear. I had never been so slow or scared on the ice before.

After warming up, I set up the cones. I dropped my lucky puck at the end of the course. Then I dragged out a single goal. I skated slowly back to the first cone. Before trying to run through the course, I stretched one last time. My plan was to try out for a college hockey team in one month. For that to happen, I had to be able to skate at full speed without pain. My trainer warned me to respect any pain that I felt. I was to stop skating if my leg hurt. Ignoring pain could lead to a re-injury. I kept this in mind as I started my run.

I began to skate. I went around the first cone slowly and smoothly. I picked up some speed around the second one. By the third cone, I was ready to turn on the jets. I pumped my legs with everything I had. I was flying through the course the way I used to! And then—I was stopping. There was a sharp pain in my leg. It happened that fast.

I took a second to stretch. The pain must have just been some rust, I thought. I skated slowly back to the beginning. Once there, I started again. When I reached top speed, the pain was back. Only this time, it was much worse. I stopped skating. Then I flung off my helmet in frustration.

Who was I kidding? I wasn't ready to make a college hockey team. I needed more time to strengthen my leg. But I didn't have time. The tryouts were in three weeks! I couldn't even get through the cones without pain. I wasn't close to ready. Plus, I wasn't as fast as I used to be. Without my speed, I was just another hockey player. Everything seemed hopeless. I had lost it.

I dropped to my knees and started to cry. My tears melted into the ice when they hit. I sat like that for about fifteen minutes. I was devastated. All my hard work was pointless. I was never going to play hockey again.

I drove around town for an hour before heading home. I walked through the door with tears in my eyes. I saw Dad standing there and looked him right in the face. "I'm ready to quit now," I said.

CHAPTER NINE

COMEBACK

The third period begins in a scoreless tie. Both teams are playing great defense. Dad used to say that scoreless games bring out the best in players. A team playing evenly for sixty minutes can lose the game in a second. He said that this fact forced guys to concentrate. One great shot or pass could change everything.

The clock ticks down to just eight minutes remaining. Every player on the ice shifts gears. I can feel this change take place. It's in the air. The crowd picks up on it, too. They rise to their feet. The pace quickens. The hits are harder than ever. Shots on goal are happening more often.

I am well rested. I have been on the bench for the last ten minutes. I watch from the sidelines as the battle continues. After an offside call on the Firestorm, we win the face-off. We spread out on offense and pass the puck around. Our hope is to bait a Firestorm defender. If he gets overeager, one of us can make a run at the goal.

We have no such luck. In fact, the opposite happens. John Simpson launches a long slap shot from the blue line. It sails wide of the net. The Firestorm now have the puck. They begin a three-on-two break. Their center fakes a pass to his right. Then he cuts back toward the middle of the ice. At the last moment, he passes to his left. The puck reaches a forward ten feet from the goal. He unleashes a one-timer!

Dave Furion never sees this laser coming. He dives left but fails to reach the puck. The black disc clanks into the left post. The pinging sound is a welcomed one. That one just missed. Dave leaps on top of the loose puck. Then the whistle blows, stopping play.

We are about to face off again. This face off is dangerous. It is deep in our zone. Coach Lewis looks down the bench. He calls me into the game. I jump to my feet. I am surprised to be called in on this very important situation. I line up on the right wing. I wait for the chance to get my stick on the puck. I want to break up the ice. I want to fly.

Six minutes remain. The crowd is screaming. They bang their feet on the floor of Elk Arena. The building is literally shaking.

The puck drops and we win the face-off. Right away, I am off down the right side. I show a burst of speed that no one can match. The puck comes my way. Just as I am about to receive it, I am checked. Although I stay on my feet, I lose sight of the puck. The fast break chance is over.

The day after feeling that pain on the middle school ice, I hung up my skates. I had officially given up on my dream. It took a while for me to come to grips with this decision. I wanted to continue fighting against the odds. My leg just wouldn't cooperate. I wasn't the same hockey player. This was a hard truth to admit.

I had worked too hard to embarrass myself at a college hockey tryout. Trying to skate on one leg wasn't worth it. College hockey players were some of the top athletes in the world. Without being 100 percent, I had no chance of making the team. Plus, there was the risk of re-injury. After skating for just a few minutes, the pain in my leg was bad. I was sure that skating for a few hours would do me in.

Three weeks later, I packed up my stuff for college. In ten cardboard boxes, I fit nearly everything I owned. We tossed my stuff into Dad's pick-up truck and headed to Minneapolis.

I didn't play hockey during my freshman year. Still, college was great. I didn't focus on the past. Instead, I looked toward a bright future. I adjusted really quickly. I loved my classes. I met lots of new friends. I even met a girl. Rachel Parker was her name. We had only hung out a few times, but she was definitely girlfriend material.

There were a few things that took some getting used to, though. Living with a roommate was hard at first. I was used to having my own space. Doing my own laundry was no fun either. Not eating homemade meals was probably the worst part. Part of me definitely missed being home.

Majoring in sports medicine was great. I was really into my classes. My major definitely made me more interested in my own injury, too. It also made me focus on my rehab twice as hard. I was getting better every day. Because of my injury, I was learning a lot. My goal was to get back to 100 percent. Not for hockey, but for myself. So I continued to work hard at the gym every day. I rode my bike around campus everywhere I went, traveling at least 10 miles per day.

When hockey season started I tried hard to ignore it. That wasn't easy though. Yes, my hockey dreams were over. But I still loved the sport. I soon realized that nothing was going to make me stop watching hockey. I couldn't help but follow the team very closely. I went to all of their home games, and a few practices as well. As a sports medicine major, I got to help the team trainers. I would treat minor injuries in the training room. I also helped a few guys rehab some bigger injuries.

At the end of one practice, I bumped into assistant coach, Pete Mitchum. He was the same guy who used to send me recruiting letters. He remembered me and my injury. He let me know that he was sorry the way things had turned out. It was a short conversation. It got me thinking thoughts that I knew I shouldn't have been thinking: *Sure, this team is really good. But they're thin at forward—having me on that right wing would make them better. I can still do it. I know I can.*

Thoughts like these took me nowhere. I would end up spending an hour replaying my injury in my head. I'd be left wondering the same thing. What would life have been like without my injury? This question often kept me awake at night. I tried hard not to think about it. I talked to my father about these thoughts. He knew all about them. I learned that the best way to deal with my injury was to focus on the future. So that's what I tried to do.

When I wasn't thinking about hockey, I was riding my bike. I rode every day during those first few months. I would pedal from my dorm room to class. That was about a fifteen-minute ride. Then I would pedal back again. My leg was starting to feel better at this point. This was great. Part of me wanted to push it. I wanted to find out what my limits were on this "new" leg. The other part of me was scared to death of another injury. This battle within my head was not resolved. Thoughts like these kept me away from the ice. At the same time, they drew me to it.

My dormitory was on the top of a really steep hill. When I left my room in the morning, I would walk my bike down it. I feared that going too fast would cause another injury. On the way home, I would walk the bike back up the hill.

There were daily races up and down that hill. People raced on their bikes and skateboards all day long. Watching these races without participating was hard for me. I have always been a competitive person. But each time I was about to try myself, the fear took hold of me. I would hop off my bike, and start walking.

By early March, my freshman year was nearly over. I was sitting in the dining hall having lunch with my roommate, Jeff. We started to talk about hockey. It was a subject I rarely got into anymore. Today was different, though. The Silver Snakes had qualified for the NCAA tournament. Jeff was talking about their first-round match-up against Michigan State College. The game was going to be taking place the next day. Everybody on campus was buzzing about it.

That conversation led into another conversation. Jeff had recently signed up for an intramural hockey league. The first game of their season also started the next day. Jeff had asked me to join the week before. I said no. Now he was practically begging me. The team was short a player. "You played hockey in high school, right, Wayne?"

"Yeah," I said, barely looking up from my lunch.

"Were you any good?" he asked. "I mean, for a little guy," he joked.

I smiled. "I was pretty good—for a little guy." Then I got serious for a second, "but I hurt my leg. So I don't play any more."

"I know all about your leg." Jeff said. "I can't play flag football—my leg. I can't go running with you guys—my leg. Your leg is fine! You ride your bike ten miles a day. I can't even ride two miles. Besides, I never see you icing it or anything. It never seems to bother you."

I tried to fake a laugh. Really, I was pretty surprised by what he was saying.

Jeff continued, "I don't think it would kill you to skate around. Besides, it's just for fun. If your leg starts to hurt, you can sit out. We've got subs."

I thought about this for a second. Beneath the table I shook my leg. I even touched it. Jeff was right. My leg felt great. It had felt great for a month or two now. I just hadn't been able to admit that to myself. Sure, the improvements were good news. But acknowledging that my leg was okay wasn't something I could do. That would lead me back to chasing my hockey dreams. I wasn't sure I was ready to do that again. But what was stopping me? Lately, *this* thought, more than any other, kept me awake at night.

Jeff looked over at me. "Hello—anybody home?"

Before I realized what I was doing, my lips moved. Two words popped out of my mouth. "I'll play."

The thought of playing hockey was too exciting to pass up. I could not deny myself the chance to play the sport I loved. Yes, my injury had changed my life. I was never going to play in the NHL. So what? That didn't mean I couldn't play hockey for fun. I thought about my father. Even with his bum leg, he played whenever he could. I buried the fear of getting injured in the back of my head.

Twenty minutes later, I was staring up at the big hill below my dorm. I hopped off my bike and started to walk up the hill. Then I stopped myself. I walked the bike back down. Once there, I hopped back on it. *I can do this,* I thought. In a few seconds, I was peddling fast and hard. I was climbing the hill quickly. There were a few other people making their way up. I passed them like they were standing still.

As I crept closer to the top, a huge smile swept across my face. I felt no pain in my leg. I reached the front door to my dorm a minute later. I didn't grab my bike and carry it up to my room, though. I raced back down the hill again. People must have thought I had gone crazy. Once I reached the bottom, I turned around and climbed back to the top. This time, I pedaled faster than before. My leg felt great! There was no pain or soreness whatsoever.

That night, I slept soundly.

The next morning was Saturday. I was supposed to meet Jeff and his friends at noon. I was so excited to step on the ice again. I was anxious to test my leg off of the bike. After all, I hadn't skated since July. That was just eight months after my injury. That was the day I officially ended my hockey career.

I laced up my skates. Then I threw on the pads and the yellow jerseys we were using. As always, I took my time lacing up my skates. Feeling the hard leather against my ankles made me happy.

When I stepped onto the ice, I was the smallest one there. Some things never change. I skated slowly around the rink to warm up. It felt great to be out there. Then I started to pick up some speed. A few seconds later, I reached top speed. Every person in the small rink was staring at me now. I didn't stop or slow down. I was flying and it was great. Every bit of speed that I once had was back—and then some.

All the work I'd done on my legs had made them stronger than ever. I couldn't believe how fast I was skating! The best news was that I felt no pain. My recovery seemed to be complete. It was as if my leg had never been broken.

I came to a stop near center ice. I sprayed snow high into the air. Jeff, and a few guys wearing yellow jerseys, stared at me. Jeff skated up to me. "Are you kidding me, Wayne?" he asked. "I've never seen anyone skate like that." He laughed. "You're like—the fastest guy in the world!"

"I bet there's somebody faster," I said, completely serious.

Jeff looked like he had just seen a ghost. "Whatever position you play, you're starting."

That game was really fun. Most of the guys I was playing against weren't really hockey players, though. They were just out for a good time. For the most part, they were amateurs. They got more than they expected that Saturday. I was every bit the same player I had been. But I was faster and stronger. Sure, I was rusty, but when I had the puck, I couldn't be caught. The strength in my legs was amazing!

After I scored five or six times, I stopped shooting. I sat on the sidelines during the last few minutes. I was staring at my leg. *Was this really happening?* I wondered.

Jeff and I went out for a burger after the game. We sat in a booth with a view of the television. The NCAA tournament was on. We didn't want to miss the Snakes' first game. I felt so happy—the happiest I had been since I hurt my leg. I was still a great player. I had lost my confidence when I injured my leg and missed last summer's tryout. After playing hockey that day, I was getting it back.

Jeff spoke to me while we both stared at the big screen. He pointed to the game. "You should be playing with those guys. You're unbelievable, Wayne."

"Thanks," I said, only half listening.

Jeff looked right at me. "I'm serious, man. You

should go out for the team next year. You'll make it."

When Jeff spoke those words, my heart raced. I shrugged my shoulders at his comment. The truth was, I was thinking the exact same thing. I reached down and touched my leg. I looked back up at the TV. I was watching the Snakes play in the NCAA tournament as we had this conversation. This was the biggest stage in collegiate hockey. I wished that I was playing too.

Maybe Jeff was right. There was no reason for me not to try out next year. I was scared, though. It had taken me all this time to come to grips with my failed dream. It was finally okay that I wasn't going to be a hockey player. I was studying sports medicine. I really liked it. Everything was going great for me. I didn't know if my heart could take being broken again by hockey. *What if I tried out and didn't make it?* I wondered. *What if I hurt my leg again?*

I voiced these doubts to Jeff. "I used to dream about playing in the NHL every day. Then I got hurt and . . . " I trailed off before finishing my thought. "When that dream died, a piece of me died. I don't know if I can go through that again. Besides," I said, "have you ever heard of a five-foot-six sophomore walk-on?"

"No," he said. Then he took a giant bite of his burger. "But I've never heard of a five-foot-six sophomore skating like you do, either. You were awesome out there today. Unstoppable!" A piece of burger flew out of his mouth.

"That's gross!" I laughed. My laughter helped calm the nervousness I was feeling. "The guys playing up there," I pointed to the TV, "are really good. They're a million times better than the guys we played against today. You know that, right?"

It was then that Jeff said something I'll never forget. "I used to be a great speller when I was a kid. Did I ever tell you that?" I had no idea what he was talking about.

"What?" I asked.

"When I was a kid, I entered spelling bees. I practiced all the time, too. I actually won for the whole state of Minnesota one year. I was a natural."

"No kidding," I said.

"In eighth grade, there was this big spelling bee at the end of the year. It was a national thing. The winners from each state competed for a college scholarship."

"Cool. So, did you get the scholarship?" I asked.

"No," he said, taking a bite of his burger. "I didn't sign up for the contest."

"Why not?" I asked.

"I figured, I'm good, but I'm not *that* good. So I sat home and watched the competition on television." Then he paused, looking right into my eyes. "I didn't spell one word wrong during that entire competition. Not one." He paused, looking up at the television set. "As funny as it sounds, that was my dream.

90

I didn't go for it, Wayne. I always regret that. If you've got a shot at this thing, you have to try. You don't want to end up thinking 'that should have been me.'"

Jeff's story was exactly what I needed to here. Before he finished talking, I knew what I had to do. "You're right, man." I said. "I've gotta go, bro." I dropped a twenty dollar bill onto the table, and ran out. "Thanks!" I yelled back to him.

I heard Jeff calling "Where are you going?" as I flew out the door.

I didn't answer him. Instead, I hopped on my bike and started pedaling. I had to get to a hockey rink. I had a lot of work to do.

CHAPTER TEN

HOCKEY DREAMS

Although the competition wasn't great, I continued playing with Jeff and his friends. I also played in a local men's league in downtown Minneapolis. The players there were much better. I got some really good practice in. I even took some hard hits. Getting checked helped me develop confidence in my leg. Each time I got hit, I would smile when I got back up. By the time summer rolled around, I barely thought about my injury.

Dad was my biggest cheerleader. I think that my comeback was more exciting for him than it was for me. His injury had ended his hockey career before it even started. When I got hurt, he often stayed up at night, wondering if our family was cursed. When I made my comeback, he realized that it was just the opposite. We were very lucky.

Every time we talked, Dad gave me a pep talk. "You've come a long way, Wayne." Dad would say, "The road was hard, and you hit some big bumps along the way. But you're still standing. I admire you for that." His words were inspirational. Every time I wanted to stop skating and rest, I would hear his voice. Those words helped drive me toward my goal.

I came home to Robbinsdale on May 15. I spent some time with Ricky my first night home. He was playing basketball at Southern Ohio College. At six foot nine, Ricky had grown another two inches since high school. His giant frame standing next to mine was a strange sight.

We went down to the arcade at the mall. It was weird being back at the local hangout, but not really being local. We both felt it, too. It was as if we had outgrown it or something. Mom used to tell me that life had a funny way of talking to you sometimes. When we stepped into that arcade, life was telling me I was getting old.

We walked over to the pop-a-shot machine. I put in a couple of quarters. I was terrible, but Ricky the basketball star, was even worse. "One year of Division I hoops under your belt, and now you stink at pop-a-shot." I laughed. "What happened to you? You used to be the master."

Ricky laughed. "My shot has improved—on a ten-foot rim, though."

I looked up at him and laughed. "If I was as tall

as Godzilla, I would have a pretty good shot too. You're basically eye-to-eye with the hoop. How hard can it be to put it in?"

"And you're so close to the ice, I'm surprised you don't freeze to it." Ricky pushed me jokingly. "Now pipe down, shrimp. I'll squash you with my size sixteens if I have to." He lifted his leg in the air. His foot was bigger than half of my torso.

It was great hanging out with Scared Stiff Rick again. As much as things had changed, they had stayed the same. Ricky told me about his experiences riding the bench at Southern Ohio. He played a total of eighteen minutes that year. Although it was frustrating, he'd learned a lot. He was looking forward to next season. I was happy for him. We talked about my return to hockey, too. Ricky said he knew I'd "be back on the ice all along." Deep down, I knew it too.

With tryouts three months away, I didn't have many chances to hang out with Ricky. Instead, I got down to business. I started heading down to Mickey's every night. I played in scrimmage games and in several leagues as well. Dad came with me a few times. He was getting too old to play for too long. I didn't tell him that, though.

By mid-June, I was playing the best hockey I'd ever played. Sure, I was still small, but I was very muscular. My balance had improved by leaps and bounds. And I could absorb a check with the best of them. My legs were like tree trunks—holding up a very small tree. This was because of all the rehab work I had done. In terms of speed, I was unmatched anywhere I laced up my skates. Opposing teams were scared of me and it felt great. I tried not to get a big head out there. After all, the players at the tryout would be much better than the guys back home.

That summer flew by. It seemed like I had just gotten home. And then I was leaving for school again. I arrived at the arena early on the first morning of the two-day tryout. In the locker room, I bumped into Pete Mitchum again. Pete was the assistant coach who had recruited me during my junior high school season. He walked up to me and shook my hand. "How's it going, Wayne?" He paused, "you here to watch the tryout?"

"No, sir." I said, "I'm here to try out myself."

Coach Mitchum looked a bit confused. "What about your leg?" he asked.

"It feels great, Coach. I've been rehabbing it for eighteen months now. I'm hoping you guys have a spot for me." I turned red in the face as I spoke.

"If you can play the way you did in high school we might."

"I'll do my best."

I played amazing hockey on that first day. Playing against the first line, I definitely held my own. In fact, I scored twice. I also proved myself to be the fastest guy on the ice. I'm sure this surprised Coach Mitchum. I hoped that my speed proved that my leg was 100 percent healthy. After all, I was still skating full speed toward the end of the day. Most players were growing tired at this point.

Of course, I was still the smallest guy on the ice. I wasn't playing like it, though. Two years away from the game had left a fire burning in my belly. Whenever I got the chance, I would lay somebody out with a body check. They tried to get me back, but most found it hard to catch me. I was simply too fast and too small.

The second day of tryouts was as good as the first. This time, I noticed head coach, Jim Morton, looking at me. Coach Morton was nodding his head and taking notes. This was a good thing, I hoped. I also hoped I wasn't about to be disappointed again.

Lying in bed that night, I tossed and turned. This was my last chance and I knew it. If I didn't get a call in the morning, my hockey career was over—again.

At eight thirty the following morning, I was awoken by the ring of the phone. I was still half-asleep when I picked it up. I jumped out of bed when I heard the voice on the other end of the line. It was Coach Mitchum. I had made the team. I couldn't have been more excited. I must have thanked him ten times. My dream was back on track!

That sophomore season was great. I played on the second line and adjusted quickly to the college game. The guys were great—even if they did start calling me Little Wayne. The nickname bothered me when I was a kid. Now I found that I liked it. I took it as a compliment. It reminded me of how hard I had fought to get here.

Being a student-athlete made keeping my grades up harder. I adjusted and managed to keep my average up. At the same time, I never missed a hockey meeting, lifting session, practice, or game. We had a good season, making it to the NCAA tournament as the number two seeded team. Unfortunately, we were knocked out in the second round.

I turned twenty-one during my junior season. At this point, I was starting to feel more grown up. Many guys my age were giving up their last two years of college to play in the NHL. Not me. My dreams had to wait until I finished getting my education. I had already seen how easily hockey could be taken away. I wanted to make sure my backup plan was in place. If and when I made it to the NHL, I would be a twenty-two-year-old rookie. By NHL standards, that was a little old. That didn't bother me.

Coach Morton offered me a full scholarship in the middle of my second season. This made my decision to stay in school even easier. Mom and Dad were very excited. I signed the scholarship papers and promised Coach Morton I wouldn't let him down.

I played great hockey that season. I led our team in assists and goals. I was a fan favorite, too. Mom said that people loved to root for the underdog. I was definitely the underdog out there. By mid-season, every time I touched the puck the crowd would scream, "Lit-tle Wayne, Lit-tle Wayne." It was pretty cool to be recognized. The crowd definitely got me fired up to play my best.

As a team, we played amazing hockey. After our first twelve games, the Silver Snakes were undefeated. Although we lost unlucky game number thirteen, we never lost again that year. Not even in the NCAA tournament, where we won a national title.

My senior year didn't offer back-to-back national championships. It was still a great year, though. I began to stand out as a top player and was even picked on the All Conference team. Being recognized in the conference was something I was very proud of. It was also an excellent way to get NHL talent scouts interested. For NHL scouts, me and my five foot six inch frame were hard to take seriously.

When that season ended, so did my college career. It had been five years since my leg injury. I felt no ill effects. I graduated with honors that May. I had a degree in sports medicine. This was a career I planned on pursuing when my hockey career ended.

On the day of the NHL draft, I waited at home. I was pleasantly surprised when I was chosen seventeenth in the second round. The team that selected me was what really excited me. I must have been the luckiest guy in the world. I was going to be suiting up for the Minnesota Elk! That was the team I had been cheering for my entire life. I couldn't have asked for anything more.

This leads me back to where I am right now. I am standing on the ice, dazed. I just got checked hard. There are five minutes remaining in a scoreless tie against the rival Chicago Firestorm. They regain possession of the puck. I drift into position on the right side.

Before I know what has happened, Dave Furion saves a hard slap shot. I never even saw that one. Dave passes it out to Alexi Kornikov, who slows things down. He waits for the rest of us to get set. We are ready to begin our attack. Less than four minutes remain now. We are well aware that this may be our final attack. Nobody wants this game to go into overtime. We want to end it now.

Alexi passes it over to me on the right side. I skate forward with a short burst, stopping in front of an eager defender. I play with the puck for a second. I am trying to keep it clear of him as I wait for someone to get open. From the corner of my eye, I can see that Alexi is making a run. I skate forward a bit, drawing the defender close. A passing lane opens up. I slide the puck past the defender's stick as he lays into me. This check nearly knocks me over.

The puck is about to reach Alexi. He is hovering in front of the goal. At the last second, it is deflected. The crowd moans as it shoots off a second defender's skate. The puck is loose. Everyone in the arena is standing. A few players are scrambling for it in front of Chicago's goal. Bodies fly onto the ice, and three sticks smack against one another. I move in closer, but not too close. I stay far enough back to defend against a possible fast break.

In the chaos, the puck shoots out toward me. I am too far out to shoot. Still, I know that the defense is expecting this rushed reaction. (I am a rookie, after all.) As the puck sails toward me, I reach back. It looks like I am about to take a big swing at the puck. I can already see the goalie staring at me. He is prepared to react to my shot. As the puck gets closer, though, I stop. I put the brakes on my swing before I make contact. This gets rid of the defender in front of me. He drops to his knees to stop my shot. But there is no shot.

With him on the ice near the right side of the goal, I skate in closer. I angle myself around the pile of players in the middle of the ice. The closer I get to the goal, the more players start to skate toward me. I move left, around a second fallen defender. I can see a small opening in the top left corner of the goal. Without thinking, I reach back and fire a shot. It looks to be on line. . .

Somehow, though, it is saved! I can't believe it!

The puck glances off the goalie's left leg. He had somehow extended his leg over his head to make the save. It flops around in front of the goal. Some-body gets his stick on it. I can't tell if it is us or them. Then the puck is loose again. I can see it to the left of the goal. It's spinning like a top. I charge it.

I am about to shoot again. But then I notice Alexi Kornikov standing unguarded on the right side of the goal. I don't turn my head in his direction. This would be a clear signal to the goalie. I would be inviting him to change his position. Instead, I lock my eyes on a spot in the back of the net. I reach my stick back. Rather than firing a shot, though, I flick a quick pass across the front of the goal. The puck squirts around the goalie's oversized stick. Alexi hits a one timer into the empty net for a goal!

The entire arena erupts! They literally explode! The red light above the goal goes off. The horn sounds. My heart feels is about to jump out of my jersey and dance. Alexi Kornikov skates over to me. "Great pass, kid!" he screams.

I raise my fist in the air and pump it. Then I look over at Coach. He is subbing in a fresh line to finish the game off. There are three minutes left. I skate to the bench to grab a bottle of water.

When I look up I realize that the crowd is chant-ing. "Lit-tle Wayne, Lit-tle Wayne." The fans in Min-nesota know me well. My parents are chanting too. Mom is crying. I nearly lose it just looking at her. The crowd stays on their feet for the next three min-utes. They keep chanting "Lit-tle Wayne, Lit-tle

Wayne" until the final horn sounds.

I glance at the glowing numbers on the scoreboard: Minnesota Elk 1, Chicago Firestorm 0. I have to smile. I'm really here—I've made it. It's an awesome moment. All of my hockey dreams are coming true.

TEST YOURSELF...ARE YOU A PROFESSIONAL READER?

Chapter 1: New Skates

Describe Wayne's first pair of skates.

Which famous hockey player is Wayne named after?

What is the name of the ice rink that Wayne skates on for the first time?

ESSAY

Think of something that you love to do. In an essay, describe the first time you ever participated in this activity. How did this new activity make you feel? Why do you think trying something new is so exciting?

Chapter 2: Little Wayne

Wayne brings his English book with him to Science class. Why did he mix up the two books?

What was Wayne's nickname? Do you think he liked that nickname? Why or why not?

What did Wayne do once he realized that he was "past the point of no return"?

Wayne gets picked on by a few of the eighth grade boys in this chapter. What did you think about the way Wayne handled being picked on? How could he have handled the situation better? What would you have done?

Chapter 3: Tryouts

How much had Wayne grown during the past year? How does Wayne measure himself?

What excuse did Ricky make up so that he wouldn't have to go to hockey tryouts? What was his real reason for not trying out?

According to Coach Nielson, why didn't Wayne make the team?

ESSAY

At the end of this chapter, Wayne says, "My big mouth had cost me big this time. It cost me a spot on the team." What does this mean? Think of a time in your life when your "big mouth" affected you negatively. Describe what happened.

Chapter 4: The Equipment Manager

In this chapter, Wayne steps onto the ice for the first time as a member of the Minnesota Elk. Which team is he playing against to open the season?

Name three jobs which Wayne was responsible for as the equipment manager.

What were some of the "little hockey details" that Wayne started to write about in his notebook?

ESSAY

In this chapter, Wayne's father says, "Your dream only dies the day you let it die." What does this quote mean? Do you think this is always true? Why or why not?

Chapter 5: Big Break

How did Wayne's flu shot save his season?

What caused Wayne to fall during his run through the cones course?

What position did Wayne play the first time he stepped onto the ice against Plymouth?

ESSAY

In this chapter Wayne is very excited to play hockey again. When he first steps onto the ice, he is over-excited and doesn't play his best. Coach Nielson tells Wayne to "let the game come to you." What do you think this means? Why can trying too hard mess you up sometimes?

Chapter 6: Teammates

Who ended up being one of Wayne's closest friends on the team? Why was this surprising?

Why did the team play worse when Darius returned?

Why does Darius thank Wayne near the end of this chapter?

ESSAY

This chapter is entitled "Teammates." Why does teamwork always beat out individual performances? Why do you think being a good teammate is so important? How is being a good teammate similar to being a good friend? Are you a good friend/teammate? Explain.

Chapter 7: Time Flies

How many assists did Wayne have during his eighth grade season? What award did he win that year?

What did Wayne think about when he felt bad about being short?

Wayne broke his leg during the first game of his senior season. Describe how it happened using your own words.

ESSAY

In this chapter, Wayne's dream is sidetracked by a bad injury. How is he feeling when he is alone in the hospital bed? Describe a time in your life when something happened and you got sidetracked. (*Hint: This doesn't have to be an injury.) How did you feel? How did you handle the situation?

Chapter 8: A Long Road

Which bone did Wayne break? Why do you think this bone take so long to heal?

When Wayne gets his cast off, is he ready to play hockey again? Explain.

What happened when Wayne finally got back on the ice after his leg had healed?

ESSAY

After reading the first eight chapters of this book, you have gotten to know Wayne pretty well. Describe Wayne's personality. Who does he remind you of? Describe how he is similar or different to this person. (*Hint: You can compare Wayne to somebody you know, yourself, or even someone on TV.)

Chapter 9: Comeback

What subject did Wayne major in during college? How did his major relate to his personal life?

Every day Wayne hops off his bike and walks it up and down the steep hill near his dormitory. Why does he do this? What is he afraid of?

Why do you think Jeff told Wayne about his eighth grade spelling bee?

ESSAY

What does the word perseverance mean? (*Hint: Use a dictionary if you need to.) Does Wayne show this quality when he decides to chase his dream again? Explain. Have you ever persevered through something difficult? Explain.

Chapter 10: Hockey Dreams

Who is Pete Mitchum?

How does Wayne feel about being called Little Wayne at this point in the book?

Which professional team drafted Wayne? Which round was he drafted in?

ESSAY

By the end of *Hockey Dreams*, Wayne has made his dream come true. He chased it down with everything he had. It wasn't easy, but it was worth it! If a book were written about you and your dreams, what would the title be? Describe this book, focusing on the beginning, the middle, and the end.